FORWARD
by FIRE

AUSTIN MOORE

Copyright © 2023 Austin Moore. All rights reserved.

This book or any portion thereof may not be reproduced or used in any manner whatsoever without the express written permission of the author, except for the use of brief quotations in a book review.

This is a work of fiction. Names, characters, events, and dialogue are the products of the author's imagination. Any resemblance to actual persons, living or dead, or actual events is purely coincidental.

Website: www.austinmoore.net
Facebook: @austinmoorebooks
Instagram: @rev.austinmoore

To all who are still on their way.

O N E

She was already getting cold.

Perhaps James imagined it as a new reality forced everything he knew into the darkness.

Finally, Gloria was gone. After eight months of fighting for her life had completely exhausted her, she inexplicably welcomed death as the cancer took her. *I'm not dying, just going home*, she kept saying. It was good enough for her.

It wasn't good enough for James. He couldn't understand how spending your life as such a selfless person and finally being rewarded with a ruthless disease and a slow, painful death could be interpreted as anything resembling a pleasant trip home—whatever home is.

He released her hand and sat beside her body, staring at her closed eyes, unable to look away, frozen in this moment, afraid to step into the next. There were no more busy monitors to draw his eyes away, no more beeping to keep him from hearing his own heart pound. He became acutely aware of the blood pulsing through his own body, the only living body in the ICU room.

James began to comfort himself with the thought that Gloria

was now in heaven where she desperately wanted to be, but his own doubt crushed the consolation before he could form a mental image. He didn't believe what she did. It was her reality—or her dream. He had attended church with her every Sunday for twenty years, but only because he never wanted to hurt her. Gloria had embraced a new spiritual world just one year into their marriage. Belief became devotion; devotion became obsession, and all that both of them had expected their marriage to be was lost. She longed for him to be like her, to know what she knew, feel what she felt; it just wasn't real to him. At first she made her case daily with fiery passion, trying to paint a verbal picture of what she believed had happened in her soul. After a few weeks she would only trouble him with occasional points of argument. After a few months and until now, all that bridged the chasm between their perspectives were her subliminal seeds of faith that were invariably met by his forest of doubt.

It was his genuine love for Gloria that kept him in church every weekend. His love had never faded. The only thought that gave him any sense of self-worth in this dismal moment was that perhaps his cooperation had meant something to her, but he knew he had withheld from her the elation that she desired most: to see her own candle of faith light his. Though for years they sat side by side in church, those chairs might as well have been in different buildings.

But I loved her. She knows that... knew that.

The smell of antiseptic steered his consciousness back into the room, and he sharpened his eyes in the low light to trace her profile, perhaps for the last time.

"I can't believe you're gone," he said through a trembling breath, sure that she was utterly gone, unable to hear his futile words from some other realm.

Mary startled him out of his haze with a gentle knock on the door. James turned and met her tear-filled, amber eyes as she slipped into the room.

"She's gone?" Her tone was even and as cold as the air.

James could only nod with his lips sealed tight and fight the lump in his throat.

Mary held his gaze with an icy glare and glided toward the other side of the bed. Only after he released a feebly attempted, unanswered smile did she turn her eyes to her mother's body. Mary leaned over Gloria, collected her lifeless hand, and studied her face. Then she glanced to every corner of the room, as if she wanted to carefully seal the moment in her mind. James sensed that Mary had left him out of this memory.

"She tried to hold on until you got here." He struggled to push his voice beyond a whisper.

Mary shut her eyes tightly. The flood of tears that washed over her cheeks were words enough for the moment.

James sat still and numb. His instincts told him to embrace her, to offer some attempt at empathy, but he couldn't move. He couldn't feel anything. He had felt her drift farther away from his heart, year after year—much like she had drifted from Gloria's faith. He never knew what to say to her, and the moment of her greatest sorrow was no different.

An eternity seemed to pass in palpable silence as Mary stood trembling. Whether she tried to hold or loose her tongue, he couldn't tell. Then, before James had even begun to search his mind for something worth saying, she was in motion and swiftly on her way.

"Mary…"

The sound of her name did nothing to slow her stride. James' voice only hurried her through the doorway. Sobs filled the hallway and faded as she rushed away. Each mournful cry took more of her father's breath.

The person James needed most lay perfectly still beside him, and the determined footsteps of his only remaining lifeline trailed out of his hearing.

No wife. No daughter. No god.

James was truly alone.

* * *

The eerie silence of the house was challenged only by the obnoxious ticking of the living room clock. Sunk deep in his favorite red chair, James wondered if Mary had chosen her best friend's house or a hotel. The six-hour drive back to university wouldn't make sense with a funeral to plan.

Who doesn't stay at home at a time like this?

Maybe he could find a way to get through to her over the next few days, but what could topple the cold, hard wall between them? He didn't even know what the wall was made of or how it had risen. Their emotional distance was a mystery that he didn't know how to begin to solve. It was clear that Mary's affection for her mother never waned, but all he had seen in her eyes for some time was indifference—until Gloria's cancer was sure to win. Then, indifference gave way to unmasked bitterness.

"I don't know if I can do this," he said to hear something other than the clock.

The fact that Mary would be forced to cooperate with him for Gloria's sake presented opportunity but gave James little hope—no hope. The only glimmer in his mind reflected off the vodka bottle on the coffee table in front of him.

He closed his eyes and flew through the corridors of his memory to find a time when he had been happy. He searched in vain, finding only moments and seasons of contentment. It had been his life's journey and deepest desire to have peace—not Gloria's idea of peace but peace of mind.

That was his dream. James never wanted to be rich. He never wanted adventure or even extravagant love. He just wanted to be okay. Enough money in the bank, enough food on the table. Just enough, with his best friend by his side, the woman who won his heart the first time he saw her.

Life married to a born-again Christian saddled him with a dull ache inside that constantly reminded him that he would never make her truly happy. She wanted more, and he knew that he would never be. What a grand expectation, that the one you chose to marry should become a completely different person, *a new creature,* she said.

Why couldn't she just be married to me and not some vision of who I should be?

After all, she was the one who changed. His life wasn't supposed to be like this. Her death wasn't supposed to leave him with mixed emotions. If she had to die, why couldn't she just leave him heartbroken and not treading in an ocean of guilt?

The bottle it is, then.

Before he could reach for relief, the front door's deadbolt creaked and turned. Mary quickly swept into the foyer and froze when she realized that her father was sitting in front of her. She turned her back and took her time shutting the heavy door, her shoulders heaving anxiously.

"Mary, I—"

"Don't." She turned to him and gulped behind locked-tight lips as her eyes darted furiously.

James sat frozen again, anticipating a flurry of words, but her tears came first. He couldn't decide if he should weather the impending storm or preempt it. His inner debate mattered little with his body fixed to his chair and his tongue stilled by fear. He wanted reconciliation, but he recognized the fire in her eyes. It wanted only to consume. Her wavy, brown hair matched her mother's, but her eyes burned like her father's when passion prevailed.

"I'm done." She exhaled slowly and stared blankly at her father.

James wouldn't risk her trademark flight before hearing more, so still he remained, though he felt he now had a grip on the present moment. He thought the tension might have a stronger grip on him.

"We'll make the arrangements. We'll get through this. Then I'm done. I'm done with you." She lowered her brows, a look of scorn coloring every line of her face.

Courage filled James' bones, and he was on his feet before he realized what he was doing. "Done with me? Just *what*, tell me, did *I* do for you to treat me like this? *What* is it that I've ever done except give you everything you need?"

"That's a great question." She cut him off. She cut him deep.

His face fell. All the thoughts he'd just gathered about respect and gratitude scattered away. Instead, he groped for a reason why she was horribly wrong, both what she said and what she thought.

All he could find with the corners of his mouth twisted in anguish was what mattered most. "I love you." Tears reinforced his sincerity.

Surely, she knows that.

"Do you? Did you love Mom? Do you really love anyone but yourself?"

Preposterous. He clenched his jaw and breathed slowly to restrain the rage that had replaced his offense in an instant.

She deepened her tone and raised her voice. "We have no real relationship. We spent no real time together. You invested *nothing* in me but money. You don't even *know* me. And I can live with that, but you weren't really there for Mom. You were just there. I didn't see love, *real love.* She deserved that. She deserved everyth—"

"I have loved you and loved your mother with all my heart, and you have *no idea* what it has cost me." His voice boomed. His anger was blind, and he couldn't measure his next words before they had escaped. "Every desire, every dream, *everything* I have wanted I have sacrificed for your mother and for you. I don't even know who I *am* anymore. God took her away from me twenty years ago, and I've been disappearing ever since. I have *unraveled* until there's nothing left. I didn't want this life, Mary, but I have loved you both *anyway.*"

He noticed his fingernails digging into his palms and relaxed his grip.

"Mary, you can't take that away from me." He sobbed into his aching hands. "It's all I have."

He fell back into his chair and wept.

Mary waited until his breathing slowed before dealing her

final blow of the night. "You can have your love then. I just wanted a father."

The knife was plunged and twisted. The door was opened and closed. She left as she arrived.

James let a moan of grief break through the silence as more tears flowed over his fingers.

How could a life filled with regret contain any more? Had he really failed his family so? Hadn't he tried?

The agony was too much to bear. The bottle was too close. The more he drank the more he cried. The more he cried the more he scanned the room. The wall of family photos, Gloria's signature decorating style, the coats on the rack by the door. Then he spotted Gloria's half-empty cup of coffee that he still hadn't removed from the bookshelf.

I can't stay here.
Wasn't this bottle full?

* * *

"How can I give *everything* and still not give enough?"

James blinked frantically, trying to remove the milky cloud from his eyes. A car flashed past him before he even noticed its approach. The raindrops that had peppered his glasses between the front door and the car weren't helping his vision. The glare stretching from the lampposts along the empty highway filled his view, and he squinted forcefully to see that the road ahead was straight.

He stilled his thoughts for a moment and found himself

focusing on the throbbing of the vein on his forehead. James was not at all fond of being angry. He valued peace over all else, so it wasn't difficult to redirect the efforts of his mind to calming down. He drew a deep, deliberate breath as another tear streaked to the corner of his mouth. The sharp lines of trees, buildings, and road signs eased back into his perception.

I'm going too fast.

He realized how heavily his foot pressed the accelerator at the exact moment he spotted the outline of a county police cruiser in the shadow of the hotel ahead. He hurried his foot to the brake pedal but kept a firm grip on the steering wheel, careful not to make it obvious that the police car had surprised him. As he passed, he was going about ten miles per hour too fast.

Oh, no. I've been drinking.

James held his breath and stared into the rear-view mirror. His hands shook. He checked his headlight setting. He clenched his teeth.

About a quarter-mile farther, he exhaled. He wasn't being followed.

How drunk am I?

His mind raced back down to his shattered heart. How could things have gotten this bad? How could Mary believe that he'd not really been a father to her? How could she think he hadn't really been there for her mom?

Sure, he'd relied on Gloria to be the relational glue of the family. But Gloria loved that role. Maybe she carried too much responsibility. Maybe he had let her do too much.

Maybe I've loved Mary through Gloria. Maybe she really needed more.

His heart sank deeper into grief. His nerves still shuddered from the confrontation. He had almost forgotten that his wife was gone. Now he was grieving the dead and the living. And what never was.

"How can I be what everyone wants me to be when I don't even know who I am?"

I've been sleepwalking my whole life.

James hadn't noticed that he'd been staring at his parking brake. He looked up just in time to see a guardrail zip into view. He froze. Too late.

It wasn't until he was airborne that his reflexes engaged in the chaos. He turned the wheel, but there was no use.

Upside down, he had time to whisper one word before the darkness took him. "God."

TWO

How bad is it?

James knew that he was alive, but he had to be in poor condition. Laying with his eyes barely closed, he waited for pain to swell into his consciousness. Nothing. He traced from arm to arm and leg to leg with his mind before timidly trying to move each as little as possible. He was surprised to find his extremities responsive, and as he breathed deeply and rolled his back, he found no discomfort at all.

What kind of air is this?

He peeled his eyes open to see a lonely cloud moving gingerly across his vision. High above, a few small white birds flitted into view, and their playful chirps joined his senses.

I must be dead.

A knot formed in his stomach. He was afraid to search out any new information, lest some kind of unpleasant end awaited him. Perhaps lying still would leave him unnoticed by the universe or any cosmic being with ill intent.

Well, I don't believe in heaven, so if I'm going somewhere…

James shuddered. Why would he be afraid of something that

isn't real? There must be an explanation.

He gathered his focus and his strength to lift his head slowly and rise to a seated position. Turning his head left and right revealed a circular tree line before and behind him and a clearing holding him at its center. He looked down and found himself resting on a flat stone, which hadn't felt hard and uncomfortable until now. Vines had crawled over and around the large rock, perhaps trying to pull it down into the ground or at least ensure that it never escaped. He wondered if this place had not been disturbed in a hundred years.

The air in front of his eyes seemed to be visible, if that could be. He could almost perceive individual luminescent particles floating about and waltzing gracefully together. Countless shimmering rainbows of microscopic size teased his attention, and waving his hand in front of his face did nothing to disturb them.

Did he have supernaturally sharp vision? Was he seeing into another dimension? Was this the afterlife?

He drew in the clean air which felt unfamiliar enough in his lungs to convince him that he was no longer on earth as he knew it. The atmosphere was cool on his skin, as if a blanket of invisible energy designed to reassure him embraced his body.

His instincts repelled the idea of comfort and stirred him into motion. He stood quickly, slid off the stone and onto the grass, and stomped around his new surroundings. This forest was remarkably dense and filled with a tall underbrush. A single walking path was cut through the woods, and an ornate but weathered stone bench stood tiredly beside the opening. The vines had no interest in it, and it seemed to shimmer as if light were trying to escape through the pores of the stone.

What is happening?

He trudged back to the stone he had awakened upon and pressed his hands firmly on it, hoping that it held some key back to reality.

This feels real. It is real. How did I get from my car to this place?

The day's events before the wreck rushed back to his mind. Gloria was gone. Mary was gone, too, but not before trying to finish him off. Loss, bitterness, and pain had made the journey with him and now fought fiercely against his attempts to process his new predicament. Regardless, this was the most peaceful place he'd ever been.

If there's a heaven, there's no way I'm there.

"So…"

James could have jumped out of his skin at the calm but unexpected gruff voice behind him. He whirled so quickly that he dizzied himself.

A man now sat on the bench that was empty only a moment ago. He was older, not old but—yes, old. Though he sat perfectly still, he struck James as agile and strong; this made no sense to him. Thick gray brows and a coarse beard disguised what James thought was the slightest smile. The man somehow appeared weathered and fresh. Seasoned and—no, he was a young man.

The stranger looked like an ordinary person, but an otherworldly unease swirled in James' gut. The man's posture was friendly but his gaze piercing.

James studied the man's unusual attire while trying to catch his breath. He was dressed like a swordsman who had just taken off his armor after a long battle. His clothing had tattered edges and patchy discoloration, giving the man the aura of a sacred scroll rolled up and set aside to tell an ancient story at a later time. His long, silver hair glistened in this alien atmosphere.

The man leaned forward and raised his brows. "Who might you be?"

James was inexplicably surprised that the man didn't already know the answer. "James." His voice wavered. "And you are...?"

The man definitely smiled this time, a bit smugly. "I don't think my name will be useful to you."

James wasn't offended by this. A sense of wisdom came with the warrior's presence and seemed to carry on his voice.

"I'm a friend."

Satisfied with this statement, James felt content to stand still and observe the man further.

The stranger looked him up and down. "I know why I'm here, but I'm not sure why *you* are. Do you know?"

James' brow furrowed. Surely if anyone was going to have answers, it would be this unusual figure. The weight of James' questions settled onto his shoulders again.

"I don't know." James tried to wear his confusion on his face but hide his mental distress. "I just know that I was in a car accident and immediately woke up here." He paused. "At least, I think it was immediate. That's what I know. There's a lot more I don't know, like... Where am I?"

The man gave his beard a single stroke. "You're where you need to be, but where you're going and what you'll find I don't know. I might have as many questions as you."

James felt even more disoriented. He grasped for mental bearings and only found another question. "Why are *you* here then?"

The man seemed amused. "That's a question I can answer

more clearly. I'm here to give you this." He produced from under his auburn cloak a piece of parchment that was folded several times and waited for James to step forward. When James didn't budge, he chuckled deeply. "I'm a friend."

James finally shuffled toward the man and took the parchment. He unfolded it carefully, but the material felt quite strong, though it appeared to be centuries old. A world written in black ink unfurled before his eyes.

"A map?" Disappointment dripped from James' words. What madness was this?

The stranger interrupted James' thoughts with a lower tone of voice. "You need this." He leaned forward as if he was ready for a fight. His thick brows covered his eyes again. "Without this, you will not succeed. You *cannot.*"

James made no attempt to disguise his doubt. "Where am I supposed to be going, and why would I want to go there when I don't even know where I am?"

The man's smile was just a memory. "Your motivation will reveal itself, I'm sure."

Before he had closed his mouth, a chill ran up James' spine. A sense of dread compelled him to look down the single narrow pathway, and through the particles, through a distant haze, he saw the unmistakable frame of his daughter Mary, shrouded in shadow. There was no doubt; she was here, too, her shoulders sunken and head hung low.

In this new world he found his voice without hesitation. "Mary!" He bellowed with more force, "*Mary!*"

Her head snapped level, and her body stood like stone.

He couldn't see her eyes, but he felt her glare wash over him. As he squinted he could see a red glow around her silhouette but couldn't make out any of her features. There was no need. He knew her physique well, and he knew how her piercing stare made him feel—as dark as the figure before him.

Mary's shoulders rose and fell, faster and faster as she breathed more heavily. She retracted her fingers into clenched fists.

This is all wrong.

James could only hear the chatter of the birds overhead. The light of the path behind Mary began to darken. The air seemed to thicken and challenge his breath.

Mary's glare remained unbroken, but a deep despair flooded James' core and took his focus. The space behind Mary filled more and more with darkness deeper than the absence of light. Menace seemed to hang over her shoulders and crawl up the path toward her. He opened his mouth to scream her name again, but nothing emerged. Fear gripped him like a python until he found no breath at all. Death approached.

The sound of hissing, cracking, and moaning crept into James' hearing and fanned the flame of his fear. The darkness gathered into twisted tentacles as it came ever closer to Mary.

She slowly but confidently turned to face the threat. And then she calmed. Her shoulders settled. Was she not afraid?

James sobbed without tears but couldn't muster the strength to say a word. He trembled with his feet rooted to the ground, helpless.

The tentacles stretched longer still and became more clearly defined in his vision. They were massive vines covered with thorns as sharp as swords, the ends weaving curiously like snakes sizing up their prey, their movement full of purpose, even intelligence. Mary's form appeared almost white against this malevolent backdrop as the darkness reached her at last.

She remained still while the hostile host of vines seized her hands and feet. They spiraled up her arms and legs and wrapped around her torso before lifting her up a few feet from the ground. Mary made no attempt to resist the attack. Suspended above the earth, she seemed to relax into the embrace of the vines as if the darkness was an old friend.

After a moment of stillness, the vines retracted swiftly and pulled her down the pathway, into the heart of the darkness. The void that had surrounded her raced after her on the ground and through the trees, the branches snapping and swaying as it passed, Mary hastening out of view.

The fear released James' heart, and he faltered down the path, finally calling out again. "*Mary!*"

With staggering velocity, light flooded the space where the darkness had been. Every trace of the terror that had taken Mary fled out of James' senses, and she vanished into the haze.

James gained speed and found a steady stride. He barreled forward, no sight or sense of the threat ahead. Desperation drove him on, but the darkness flew away from him too quickly. The path veered left. An opening peaked around this bend. He ran as fast as he had ever run, tears streaming down his face. He was ready to die for Mary.

He held his breath as he burst into the clearing and stumbled to an awkward halt to keep from running into a large stone. The stone. The clearing.

James was back where he had begun.

What? No.

He gasped and leaned over the stone. Fresh sobs threatened to take him, and he buckled onto the rugged surface.

Then overwhelming relief gripped his mind and stayed his tears.

It has to be.

Nothing that had happened since he'd awakened in this place was plausible.

The air, the darkness, the thorns, Mary—

"You're not dreaming."

James seized and fell in a twisted heap on the ground.

The man.

James scrambled to his feet, deciding to pretend that he hadn't been scared half to death.

He didn't bother to gather his breath but panted through his reply. "No, I'm dreaming. There's no other explanation. I'm unconscious in my car, in a hospital bed, in a ditch—I don't know. *This* is great dream material. This is guilt and grief and issues I should probably see a therapist about manifesting in my poor bruised and broken mind. I'm a broken man at the edge of sanity." He wiped his cheeks and nodded in agreement with his own assessment. "Nothing like this could be real."

He began to pace frenetically with his eyes fixed on the warrior as his analysis bolstered his confidence. "You're not real, old-young man. You're the Gandalf my brain needs to process my way out of a nervous breakdown. *This* is not happening. My daughter wasn't just taken by vines and swallowed by a demonic black hole, and I'm not stuck in some magical woods with an exit that's actually an entrance! Where I'm from, you can't *see the air, man!*"

When he finished, he was standing almost nose to nose with the stranger, waiting for confirmation, still gasping.

No expression graced the man's face. "You're welcome to

your theories."

James had half-expected to wake up after his speech. He had tried pinching himself a moment ago. How could he get out of this place?

The man stood like a regal statue, unfazed by James' closeness.

Okay, now what?

"Now..." Did the man smile? "You go find her."

James stared at him until his breathing calmed, and the conviction in the man's eyes forced James to consider his words.

"Find her," he said back to the warrior.

Find her. Chase a nightmare within a nightmare to save a dream that's long dead.

James didn't know what else to do, and his patience was thin. "Maybe the only way out of this sick joke is to play along. Fine. Apparently, I have time." He stepped back and waited for instructions with his hands on his hips, but none came.

The man glanced down at James' right pants pocket and back up to his eyes.

James held his gaze while he removed the map that he didn't remember pocketing. He only looked down when it was fully opened. With his eyes he roamed the page over forest, river, mountain, and valley. Then he noticed a small forest clearing with a stone at its center. James looked up and all around himself. The man was gone.

THREE

James tightened every muscle in his body and released the scream that he'd suppressed in the man's presence. It left his ears ringing.

He flicked the map out of his sight, and it fluttered to the ground. He stood motionless for a few moments with his eyes fixed on the space between him and the trees, even ignoring the living air ducking in and out of his view.

Before deciding how to proceed, he had to free himself from the crossroads in his mind. His fresh grief called him down a road of lament. Regret and loss echoed to him from the past. He didn't want to walk that path, but he wanted to escape the alternative. Forward. No, the only way forward was toward a door that was closed, locked, and burned to ash. He would only find more pain forward, along with an impossible task that would prove him a failure again.

"Find her," he repeated. "I don't think she'd like that." He hung his head. "I don't think I can do that."

He decided that the man's instructions indicated that she was alive in this world. A man who could disappear was probably a reliable source. He shook his head at the absurdity of what had happened in the last few minutes.

As he replayed Mary's disappearance in his mind, he could feel her gaze again. The way she looked at him in the hospital, in his home, on the path—she didn't want saving. What could be more clear than the way she stood still while a dark force dragged her into the mouth of a living hell?

He lowered his eyes to the map again.

I have to do something other than stand here forever.

He bent low, swiped the map, and slapped it on the stone in one motion. "I may be dreaming. I may be in hell. I might have constructed a prison of guilt in my mind—a fine move that would be. I might be slumped in a wheelchair in a mental hospital right now, but I'm not giving up yet. Even a mental prison can be escaped." He located the clearing again on the map. "I've got to at least try to find a way out of this."

James lined up the stone on the map with its position in the clearing. "This can't be right, old man." The only path leading from the clearing was south, and the only path on the map was north. "Great. Guess I'll have to figure this out on my own." He spun around and started. The southern path and the bench had vanished.

James sighed. "Ah, yes, of course. More disappearing. Beautiful."

Sarcasm gave way to the rage that stirred again in his gut. He lifted the map in front of him and gathered his hands at the top to tear it in half when shimmering wisps of energy began to lift from the page. The spectacle unfolding before him resembled streams of blue smoke with its edges traced by orange flames. The burning smoke swept over the parchment and lit every line of ink in a captivating display of dangerous beauty. As the fire teased at his fingers, James realized that he hadn't flinched. No threat had entered his mind or triggered his reflexes. Only a subtle warmth transferred from the map to his hands. Pure amazement held him speechless.

The gaseous embers pulled his focus upward, drifting north. They pulsed in glowing, swirling waves, ebbing toward the path that the map promised but his eyes denied. The map called him forward with nowhere to go.

Still, he couldn't keep from walking toward the living light. The closer he stepped to the trees, the more vibrant the colors, orange and blue, and the more boisterous their movement. He stopped about a foot from the wall of branches and brush, unable to see through to an answer to this riddle.

James sighed again, closed his eyes, and leaned forward to rest his hand on a branch and think, but he staggered forward, having missed the rather thick branch. He awkwardly straightened again and massaged his lower back while the flames danced wildly. Confusion and frustration twisted his features.

"I thought that branch was lower."

He reached forward again to touch the branch and jerked backward with a gasp as the branch lifted straight up to avoid his hand. He tweaked his back properly this time and bent double to relieve the pain and decide if back pain or moving trees was more of a nuisance.

"Nope," he whispered a few dozen times. This was too much.

The chirping of the white birds sounded a lot like laughter.

He stretched up slowly again and stared forward through the floating fire.

"A magic map and moving trees…" He shook his head briskly

and snorted a strong breath. "I'm already in for a pound."

Abruptly, James strode forward with a lengthy gait and one eye open. Tree branches and thick, tangly brush and vines unwove and slithered out of his way. Roots burrowed, trunks leaned, and grass sprung up under his feet. The forest hurried away from him. A new path formed without delay. With each stride, the trail unfolded from thin air and made sure to stay a few feet in front of him. Wood, stone, and soil bent before the map's unnatural will.

James gained more confidence as he marched on, and he began to chuckle, louder and louder until he roared with laughter, all doubt behind him in the clearing. Smoke and flame waltzed all around him and flew farther forward like a grateful flock of uncaged birds.

"There's no way I came up with this nonsense!"

After a few more of James' proud steps, the path widened and unrolled furiously before him as far as he could see, and the guiding fire dove back into the map, leaving only a faint glow in the rich black ink.

James stopped and held his breath while he stared into the now-dormant parchment. In a few seconds he heard the swell of a great variety of bird songs and animal chatter, all jubilant and wonderful, all seeming to celebrate his arrival. He exhaled with a deep laugh and spun to take in the sight and sound of a forest teeming with life. Trees, flowers, and stones of many shapes and colors delighted his eyes as they flourished into place, miniscule flashes of light sweeping and soaring around each petal, leaf, and blade. The branches overhead bobbed and swayed with the playful activity of myriad birds and creatures.

James stood and drank in the living picture. The air seemed

cooler and his lungs more eager to take it in. The grass and flowers smelled sweet but utterly bizarre.

"This is no hell."

A happier moment he couldn't remember. When he tried, he quickly brushed the train of thought from his mind to avoid chasing away this new feeling. He lingered in his thoughts only long enough to acknowledge that marching blindly through the forest was the bravest thing he'd ever done.

He lifted his face and felt the warmth of the sun, but no sun shined overhead or stretched through the trees. No matter. He embraced his new surroundings with ignorant bliss and stretched his back again, only this time like a man preparing for further exercise.

He gathered his focus to the new path that had just unrolled ahead of him and wondered what could be around the far-off bend to the right. He took a single step and froze. The bliss waned as Mary's face crossed his mind again. Here he was without her, finally feeling happy. Who knew where she was and what horrors may hold her captive? They had gone in opposite directions once again. Once again it had seemed out of his control.

James thought of her smile; he didn't know when he'd last seen it. He remembered holding her and weeping over her on the day she was born and how he'd promised with trembling whispers to take care of her.

The bliss was gone. No comforting thought remained, but a long, deep breath swept him forward down the path at a brisk pace. "She might not want to be saved, but what kind of father wouldn't try?"

Scattered stepping stones gradually replaced the grass beneath him until he traveled a rugged roadway of neatly arranged granite plates, clearly placed with care. He resisted the urge to mutter a quip about "The Wizard of Oz," with Mary's fate hovering over him like a cloud. This world may only exist in his mind, but the burden of high stakes and grave danger rested on his heart. What if helping Mary was the only way out? What if the man—real or imagined—was right about what he must do? So far, he seemed to be right about the map.

As the road bent right, it widened a bit. New foliage peppered the landscape. He didn't recognize a single tree or flower, but he felt at home. A few friendly creatures resembling chipmunks scampered up and down the trees and over the branches, paying no attention to James. He noticed one gathering dark, round berries from a thin, yellow vine. Tiny blue birds darted across the path before and behind him with multi-toned whistles. He thought he heard a deep lowing from some nearby creature.

A rich ecosystem thrived here, and none of it posed a danger to him, something he knew instinctively. Without a pressing objective, his curiosity would have drawn him from the path to investigate every unfamiliar feature of the woods. Animals resembling foxes, frogs, and snails kept his head in constant motion.

Around twist and turn, other paths of dirt, grass, and stone broke from the roadway and through the forest. James didn't wonder if he should take any of them. None of them seemed attractive or threatening. He somehow knew they simply weren't for him.

After passing a few trails, he glanced down at his right pocket and noticed tiny wisps of smoke streaming forward before he could even reach for the map. At least he had a reliable guide, albeit silent. He imagined that his destination must be far from this whimsical place. Nothing as sinister as the vines that took his daughter would make its home somewhere so serene.

"I hope I can show this place to Mary." He hadn't measured his words before he uttered them and sank his own heart again. His soul ached in protest of the emotional path that wound much more dramatically than the one carrying James' feet.

Hope. What a foreign idea to infiltrate his mind and pound on the door of his doubtful heart. James had brimmed with hope as a young man seeking a steady career and peaceful life with his sweetheart. He had been driven to reach a solid foundation, sure footing for a contented and fruitful future. He had wanted the whole picket-fence scenario, the kids, the dog, the college and retirement funds; it was all anyone needed. The American dream was his dream, but the pursuit of happiness was short-lived after college.

Who knew that marriage would be the death of his desires? His journey had ended as soon as it had begun. How could he have known? One would think that over a two-year engagement he would sense Gloria's religious leanings. There were none. Gloria was a good person. She was kind, thoughtful, and generous to a fault. She would always give more than she received, and it never bothered her when others took too much.

But faith was something different. It came out of nowhere, and then her good heart wasn't enough. A normal life wasn't enough. James wasn't enough. Gloria had gone from a deep desire to accommodate her new husband to a deeper desire to change him. He never wanted to change.

Maybe I should have tried.

The sound of Mary's voice snapped him out of his musing

and halted his steps. Softly she rambled in an argumentative tone, as if pleading her case in a courtroom. She was far enough away that her words were imperceptible, but she had to be close by. A slender path jutted to the left, and when James whipped his head in that direction, her voice became a little louder. He didn't think. He darted down the slender track. He ducked under knotty branches and pushed aside unfriendly fronds, struggling to hear above the twigs and leaves that snapped and crunched beneath him. The path wound wildly, taking him through thorny leaves and over rocky terrain. Branches scraped at his arms and face. Sharp stones threatened to pierce the soles of his shoes. At last the path disappeared into a tangle of sticks. Her fading voice compelled him farther.

I'm losing her.

As her muttering grew more faint, her tone grew more distressed. He stomped his own trail and hacked through branch and brush, his arms flailing.

She's just ahead.

Were trees leaning to impede him? Were roots squirming to trip him? He wouldn't be slowed. He couldn't be stopped. He would do anything for Mary.

A yellow light ahead gave him a target. He groped with his arms and legs in its direction. Mary sobbed. He had to catch up. Only a thick wall of reeds held back the glow. He burst through with a groan and lurched into a blinding light which forced him to cover his eyes with his arms while his pupils adjusted. He squinted and scanned left and then right. No sobbing. No voice at all.

He staggered about and called her name loudly. He called again with a more apologetic tone.

James stilled himself and breathed deeply, waiting to learn anything with his eyes or ears. His eyes focused before he heard a sound, and his jaw dropped. In front of him a vast meadow spread over gently rolling hills. Patches of wildflowers dressed in brilliant neon colors meandered through the landscape. A placid lake rested in the distance. The scene was even more beautiful than the path he'd just traveled. But Mary wasn't in sight.

As he plodded deeper into the meadow, James called out Mary's name over and over until it was just a whisper. He stopped and then shook until tears became sobs. Her distraught voice echoed in his mind and dragged his heart deeper in his chest.

"Hello?"

Was that a voice?

James held his breath and cocked his head.

"Hello? Is somebody there?" rolled a subtly southern dialect on a soft breeze.

FOUR

Over a hill James spotted someone's head bobbing up and down. A young man emerged through a patch of yellow flowers, trotting in his direction. James jogged toward him, wiping the tears from his face.

Maybe he saw her!

The man shouted, "Hello!" just before tumbling headlong down the other side of the hill and vanishing into another patch of flowers. The thud sent hundreds of lavender butterflies whirling upward and scattering through the meadow, a mesmerizing display that managed to soothe James' nerves. The awkward stranger raised a single thumb to signal his condition before springing to his feet and wobbling on. He raised his eyebrows high to greet James, and his pitch-black hairline rolled backward to make room for them.

They slowed to a walk and met with a firm handshake. The man's fit frame was as sharp as his cheekbones. James had never seen eyes so green or skin so copper.

"What brings you here?" said the man with a wide, thin smile and great enthusiasm.

"Have you seen a young woman?" Pleasantries would have to wait. "Let's see, she's about—"

"Oh, I've not seen anyone but you, friend."

"I followed her voice here, so she must have come by. Are you sure you didn't notice anything?" He was sure to convey urgency in his tone and to wear it plainly on his face.

"I only heard you. I'm afraid I've not crossed paths with Mary."

James felt a jolt, and his hair stood on end. "How did you—" Then he remembered that he'd been calling her name and cut himself off before embarrassing himself. "How did you get here?" He fought to calm his nerves again.

"Here in this beautiful meadow?" The young man's eyes twinkled. "Now that's a real question." His smile stretched even wider and then immediately fell. "I came here looking for something." He gazed through James to another time. "I was trying to be something... be someone, really. I didn't get where I was trying to go, but I found something better." He raised his smile again and spun with his arms wide, gesturing to the whole meadow. "Have you ever seen a place like this?" He emphasized every word.

"I admit I haven't. It's breathtaking." James decided to grant his acquaintance a little patience and look around again.

The meadow offered more than a view; it was a feast for the senses. Some of the butterflies that the man had displaced still fluttered about, looking for new resting places. Their wings reflected the source-less light into a metallic sparkle. The flowers around him dripped with deep color. They sent a sweet perfume on a soft, whistling breeze.

"So you live... here?"

The man leaned closer with a sprightly grin. "Come with me."

The man turned on his heel and marched toward the hill he'd tumbled down. James reluctantly followed, darting his eyes left and right for a trace of Mary's presence. After a few steps, the man halted mid-stride and spun around again. James almost ran into him, jerking to a stop.

"Please forgive my manners! I just realized I didn't introduce myself or ask your name," the man blurted.

James took a step back. "I'm James."

"James, I am Zell, and it really is a pleasure to meet you." Sadness washed over his face. "It really has been a long time."

Off marched Zell again at a quicker pace.

That didn't sound creepy at all, Zell.

James jogged to keep up with him on the upward slope. As they crested the hill, the meadow proved to be larger than James had been able to see at first. From the edge of the lake, an easy grade crawled down to a small flat. At the center of the flat stood a lonely tree like an oak determined to stretch its branches as far outward as its roots would allow. Each branch rolled and rose and dove with playful exploration, crossing each other here and there. James pried his eyes from the strange tree and traced the outline of the meadow, which was carved out of dense woods like an oasis. No birds sang here. Perfect quiet prevailed beyond the breeze. James wished that Mary's voice would emerge again.

Zell headed for the lake, glancing over his shoulders occasionally to check James' pace and offer another reassuring grin. Only now James noticed that Zell wore slacks and a button-up shirt, not some mysterious medieval or ancient garb like his teleporting friend from the clearing. Only shoes were missing from his attire.

Down the grassy hillside they hiked, winding around the wildflowers. James drew a final full breath of perfume as the flowers gave way to open grassland. His acquaintance led on, swinging his arms wide with an almost comical confidence.

A sandy beach bordered this side of the lake. Zell approached it like a child on vacation and dug his toes into the sand on his way to the crystal-clear water. James approached with little interest. Mary's fate dominated his thoughts.

"Notice anything about this water?" Zell said, a little too loudly.

James rubbed his eyes and studied the lake. It was unclouded, pristine. The peaks and valleys of the lake's floor were laid bare. Cool blues and greens painted the rolling stone under the surface. But there was something more. James wrinkled his forehead to enhance his powers of observation.

"The water isn't moving." James stared with his mouth agape.

It didn't move at all. No ripples on the surface, no surge or swell on the sand. Even as a fresh gust of wind whisked through the meadow, the reeds along the far-side bank bowed while the water stood like stone.

James stepped close and bent low to swipe the surface. He drew back a wet hand, but the lake remained undisturbed. He shook his head and blinked wildly. His fingers dripped over the surface, and each drop returned without the slightest splash. He noticed one more oddity that he decided not to point out: the clouds overhead and a wandering butterfly reflected off the surface, but James did not.

How could—

"This lake is pure peace, my friend. It's what I could never find before." Zell zoned out again with his arms folded. "The expectations of others ate at me. I used to care more than anything about what they thought. Everyone depended on me. They *needed* me. And I needed them to need me." He dipped his head to pry James' eyes from the stationary water. "But they never *really* saw me. They never *really* appreciated what I sacrificed, how I poured my life out for others. They just kept taking and taking, and what *I* wanted... was always this."

Zell hovered his hand over the water. "I was good at hiding it, but from the surface to the deepest part of me, I never had rest." He gestured dramatically. "I passed through this meadow in search of the strength to be *even more* for someone else, but when I found this lake... I found myself. I found the *real* answer I was looking for." He looked deep into James' eyes and nodded. "It was time to take care of me."

James' heart ached for his own troubled waters.

"So!" Zell's smile slashed across his face again. "Therapy!" Zell dashed away from the lake and onto the grass again. He turned back and skipped into a full sprint toward the lake. He bounded through the sand and planted his feet just before the edge to launch himself into a high, arcing dive. After soaring gracefully through the air, he didn't hit the water so much as he passed through it without a sound.

James flinched, expecting him to land head-first on the bottom, but the water provided enough resistance to allow him to breaststroke away from the beach. Downward he swam to the middle of the lake's floor.

James scratched his head. "Swimming through glass. Yeah, my brain is just fine. Clearly, they're getting my meds right."

After reaching the bottom, Zell stood up straight, turned, and waved politely at James, who weakly returned the gesture. Then Zell took off running as if there was no resistance at all, dodging around and leaping over rocks. He somersaulted or vaulted over every obstacle below and then gained speed and sprinted around the shallow edge of the large bowl, making several laps without coming up for air.

James' jaw eased lower as Zell further demonstrated his agility and lung capacity.

Is this the guy who ate a face-full of flowers a few minutes ago?

Back to the surface Zell finally swam. He broke the surface without a gasp—just calm, even breath. He treaded with his hands and feet like a hummingbird on air.

"Well?" Zell nodded his head back, a clear invitation into the strange water.

"Uh—" James palmed the outside of his right pants pocket. "I'll have to pass."

"No worries." Zell paddled back to the shore and out of the water as still as ice. He dripped from head to toe as he passed over the beach and strolled down the slope toward the flat. James followed, politeness his chief motivation.

He tried to process the anatomy of the tree ahead and found it boggling. The tree needed remarkable strength to hold its branches so far from its trunk. The branches didn't seem to sag or bow but wandered wherever they pleased. James decided that the roots stretched deep and the wood was incredibly dense, unless more supernatural power was at work.

Zell let the breeze carry his words over his shoulder. "You know, this place has changed since I arrived—the meadow. The hills have shifted, the flowers changed colors. There used to be more trees, but I've never cared for woods. The butterflies weren't here; I've always loved butterflies. And this…" They passed through the outer branches of the majestic tree. "This has become my home." Zell plucked a dark blue plum-like fruit as large as his fist and took a fierce bite. The fruit's transparent juice burst out and ran down his arm. "Everything I need is here. Everything is as I desire," he mumbled with his cheeks stuffed.

James thought it a bit rude that he wasn't encouraged to take a fruit of his own, but he didn't feel hungry. *Can I get hungry here?*

They weaved and ducked their way around the mighty branches to the tree's massive trunk. Zell plopped himself on the ground with his back against the sturdy pillar in a space that seemed to hug his body.

"The night I came here, I sat in this spot and wept until I couldn't weep anymore. I had been chasing after the needs of people who never listened to me, who never saw *my* needs. Then this tree listened." Zell seemed to search James' face for disbelief. "After I had spent every ounce of my energy wallowing in woe and despair, I simply said, 'I just wish I had a place to sleep.'" As soon as he had uttered these words, the closest branches jolted to life and slithered in sync to form a roomy hammock with a bed of leaves, suspended waist-high and swaying gently. A few leaves fluttered to the ground—casualties of the tree's hasty accommodation.

Again, James didn't want to believe his eyes; He shook his head and huffed. *Why not?*

After standing, Zell flung his legs out from under himself and spun his body into a barrel roll before landing perfectly in the center of the hammock. It caught him like a glove receiving a baseball and bobbed to a stop. Zell smirked with his hands behind his head, taking in James' unveiled awe.

James raised one eyebrow and squinted at Zell. "You, um... You weren't quite so graceful when we met."

Zell snickered. "Oh, I was a little nervous! It was a real shock—a good one—to have a guest. You know..." He sent his eyes through the tree's crown and waxed poetic again. "The only rain on my perfect parade here is that I never get to share what I have. I would love to know that others have this kind of tranquility. It's changed my life, James. I have perfect peace and not a soul to preach it to." He looked back at James and softened his expression. "I'm glad you came, friend."

"I'm grateful for your hospitality. And it's nice to know I'm not alone here." Mary's desperate voice entered James' thoughts again and sent a fresh wave of anxiety through his body. He tried to convey regret, drawing back his cheeks. "I just have to find my daughter."

Zell gazed up again. "Some shade would be nice." With a swish, the leaves and branches overhead plugged every space that allowed light rays to fall under the tree.

James shook his head yet again. Why did something so fantastic make him feel so uneasy?

"Friend, if you keep shaking your head like that, it just might fall off." He smiled kindly, his green eyes glowing under the newly formed shade. "Tell me about Mary."

His heart moaned in his chest. He dropped his shoulders and looked at the ground. "Mary is a long story. She's everything to me." He blinked away a tear. "But I think I've ruined our relationship."

"Now, James, relationships require two."

"A girl needs her father," James rattled off more forcefully than he intended. He pursed his lips and exhaled his frustration. "She needed more from me. I have spent her whole life resenting her mother for loving a God that I didn't."

"*Ooh, heavy stuff.*" Zell swung his legs over the side of his hammock and sat straight up.

James struggled to bolster his weakening voice. "I was there. But I wasn't there. I punished my wife for her faith by withdrawing from the moment. *Every* moment. I can't remember the last time I actually showed her that I loved her. I just ate, slept, worked, and zoned out. I was so angry." James couldn't believe what he was saying. "I was hurt, and I hurt my wife. Why was I so cold to her?"

"You were being true to yourself."

James didn't even hear Zell. "I was so cold that I didn't give Mary the father that she needed. I *actually* pretended that she didn't need me. What kind of dad checks out on their kid? What kind of husband hates a wife who loves him? Why did I hate God so much?"

"You couldn't live a lie!"

"It's not a lie!" James staggered back, blinking furiously. "It's true," he said, more to himself than to Zell. The tears coating his cheeks were as smooth as the lake behind him. "I know it's true. I saw it every day. Gloria's love was nothing ordinary. It was from God. It *was* God. It was patient and kind. It was so strong." He trembled in sync with his wavering breath. "God knows I put it to the test."

James looked at the ground and clenched his fists, firmly gripping the truth he'd avoided for years.

You're real.

Wondering if this was the first time he'd actually prayed, he looked up and found unmasked annoyance on Zell's face.

"So, what's in your pocket?"

The question pierced James' gut. "I'm sorry?"

"Whatever is in your pocket kept you out of the lake. I've gotta say, James, I was a little offended." Zell's smile sprawled back into place.

"Oh, I..." James' eyes shifted back and forth like a typewriter carriage gathering the pros and cons of answering the question. The strange man in the clearing hadn't instructed him to keep any secrets, but James pushed past a thin wall of apprehension.

I guess there's no harm.

"It was a gift from a friend." He reached into his pocket.

"I thought you chased all your friends away," said Zell before rolling backward and shooting his feet into the air, cackling loudly.

Anger snapped awake within James. He set his teeth together and stared with blank countenance at the space where Zell's eyes would land when he rolled back upright.

Zell sat up and laid his smile down like a weapon. "Oh, friend, you must forgive my cavalier remark. I've always loved a good zinger, and the opportunities are few and far these days."

James held his glare for a few seconds to make his offense clear. After producing the map, he began to unfold it, ignoring Zell's outstretched hand. When the map was fully opened, Zell was peering over his shoulder after a quick scramble from his hammock. James stood with rigid shoulders, resisting the urge to shrug him off.

His irritation was replaced in an instant by concern. James found no glow in the lines of the map. He studied every corner for a hint of smoke or fire. He stretched his grip wide in search of the warmth that he'd noticed in the clearing. Nothing.

Zell smacked his lips and walked in front of James. He casually waved the back of his hand at the map. "Yeah, I've seen one of those before. Not very useful if you ask me."

James refolded the parchment, careful not to indicate his surprise that he found no sign of its supernatural properties. "Well, now you know what's been in my pocket," he said curtly.

Zell leaned against the trunk and flashed another smirk. "You've been following that, haven't you?"

James' eyes widened. He had forgotten. "I didn't follow it here." He was off the path, and now he felt like the meadow's butterflies had made their home in his stomach.

"Well, that's just proof the best map is your own instincts."

"It was Mary's voice. That's why I left the path I was on. I know I heard her."

I had to follow her voice.

"And her voice was gone the moment you found this place, correct?" Zell's cheeks crowded his smiling eyes.

James frowned. "What are you getting at?"

"Well..." Zell relished a dramatic pause. "Call me crazy, but is it possible that Mary wanted you to find this place? Like, maybe you're all worked up over finding her, but she really just wants you to be happy?"

What?

"What if, James, your map was leading you to her, but *truth* was leading you to a place of rest? What if that map wasn't taking you where you really need to go? Maybe—just *maybe*—all this holding on you're doing isn't really what's best for anyone, and it's time for you to let go."

"No." James didn't hesitate. He was on the right path, and then he left it.

This is all wrong. Peace isn't in this place; peace was on the path.

"I've got to get going. I'm off track." James held his feet still long enough to make his leave politely. "It's been nice meeting you, Zell."

Zell studied James' eyes carefully. "Are you sure?"

"I'm sure."

Zell beamed like a proud father, stepped close, and slapped James' shoulders. "The best peace is when you're sure that you're sure that you're on the right path. I know you're gonna find her, James. I've got faith in you."

James closed his eyes and breathed in the cool breeze. Things were becoming clear. Mary was going to have a father who loved her and fought for her, even if it was too late.

Things are changing… and I think I'm changing.

"It's been fun," Zell said, but from a distance.

James opened his eyes and turned his head to spot him standing outside the tree's reach with his hands on his hips. How had he gone so far so quickly?

The ground rumbled with increasing intensity, and before James could react, thick roots burst from beneath the earth all around him. Like eels they weaved and wriggled skyward, forming a perimeter around him. He heaved forward through falling dirt, dodging the branches and twisting sideways to slip between two roots, but the space was too small when he arrived. He bolted left and followed the roots to find an opening.

"You're wasting your time, James," Zell called.

James stopped and swiveled his head. No way out. The

canopy's branches lifted and then spread downward to intertwine with the roots. A spherical prison was taking shape, trapping him inside.

"What are you *doing,* Zell?" James roared. His lungs worked furiously to keep up with his burst of energy and his climbing rage. The vein in his forehead throbbed.

"Friend, I don't think you know what's good for you."

The rays of light within James' new cell grew thinner. The leaves scurried to complete a chamber of darkness. In a moment James panted with his hands on his knees in total blackness.

"What you *need...* is rest."

"I *need* to get away from a psychopath, apparently!" James snarled.

"You should be careful how you speak to me, friend." Zell exaggerated his southern drawl. "I hold the keys to your current confinement."

Now what? James' gripped the sides of his head.

That's it!

"I really wish I could get out of here." James winced and hoped that the tree would respond to his desire.

"Now, James, I told you the tree listens to *me*." Zell chuckled quietly.

James flinched and threw his neck back. Zell's voice was coming from above him.

As he looked up, faint, green light emanated from a multitude of tiny pollen-like particles falling softly. The canopy was a starry sky over a dense fog, interrupted only by Zell's wiry silhouette. Leaves began to drift and lilt across James' vision, and his eyelids drooped lower in time with their hypnotic rhythm.

"*Rest*, James."

He shook his head violently and crouched low. *Think, James!*

"Getting sleepy, friend?"

The map! James groped for his pocket. Drowsiness dulled his strength as he reached in and dragged out the parchment. He unfolded it recklessly. Still no glow. The leaves spun faster. *I need help.* The dust settled on his skin. A strange smell tugged at his attention. *Mary.* The darkness rolled over his eyes. His grip on the map loosened. His bones gave way, and as he fell face-first he mustered the strength to shout the name. "*Jesus!*"

Orange and blue light exploded in every direction from the map with the force of a hurricane. The dust and leaves vaporized. Branches snapped and severed. Roots recoiled underground. Scattered thuds thundered all around.

James' ears rang from the blast. His head pounded. He pried one eye open, the other pressed against the ground. He begged his senses to sharpen until he could finally focus his eye.

There lay Zell crumpled several yards away, unconscious, with a large branch pinning his legs. James rolled onto his back to see only the tree's massive trunk twisted into a hook, twitching.

I've gotta get out of here.

F I V E

James dragged himself upright and almost fell again scooping up the map. Wisps of flaming smoke swirled to life and flowed beyond the tree toward the far side of the flat. Zell drew a sputtering breath that raised the hair on James' neck. He needed no more invitation to leave. He stomped toward the tree line with all his might, folding the map as he went. There was no path ahead. Not yet. James locked his jaw and extended the map. Its energy flowed farther ahead.

"Get the map!" followed a whimpering cry.

James released a low-pitched yell that reached peak volume as he barged into the forest. The trees fled his presence, and the soil and rocks paved under his feet. The forest popped and buckled in haste.

The ground rumbled, threatening his stride, buckling his knees as he clamored down the unfolding path. The wounded tree still obeyed its master. Dirt and pebbles soared over his head and landed in front of him. He looked over his shoulder in time to see roots erupt out of the path floor and stretch after him.

"Nope, nope, nope, nope…" An opening wasn't far ahead.

"God, I can't think of a better time to chat." Another root shot up beside his foot. "I need You to save me." The end of a root zipped over his shoulder and snapped at the map. "Whoa—and I don't just mean save me from an angry tree." He loped left and then right over cracks in the earth. Another root swiped in front of his face. He ducked and rushed on. "But definitely save me from the murder tree!"

The ground beneath him waved like a whip and vaulted him high into the air. He passed out of the forest airborne, the edge of a cliff just ahead. James screamed as his feet went over his head, and he tucked in time to roll on his back and tumble wildly. He kept his arms and legs close to his body until he flopped onto his back near the cliff's edge.

His vision spun, and his stomach turned. Pain shot through his joints, but urgency set him back in motion. In desperation he sat straight up with the map stretched out in front of his chest just as the roots arrived from the ground and the sky, all thrusting at him. A fierce, fiery blast of light flashed from the parchment and sent shards of wood flying. He covered his head as fragments rained all around him. He looked up and watched what was left of the roots writhe and withdraw into the ground and up the path.

James gasped for air. The forest lay still. Warmth radiated from the still glowing map.

The dust settled, revealing a lanky figure standing far off on the mangled path he had just survived. Zell. James scrambled to his feet through aching pain and faced the cliff. There was nothing but a white haze as far as he could see beyond its edge. Blue smoke and orange flame from the map beckoned into the mysterious fog. No path around the forest left or right. The fire licked forward in steady waves, begging his action.

James glanced back. Zell walked toward him with raised shoulders and clenched fists. James stepped close to the edge and peered down. A chasm awaited below. Deep darkness was ready to swallow him.

I can't go forward.

He turned and faced Zell, who was now jogging down the path, evading fallen branches and furrowed earth. The map's energy poured around either side of James, as if trying to drag him toward the abyss.

What do I do?

James closed his eyes, and the sound of rushing water eased into his consciousness and calmed his breathing.

Water?

He opened his eyes. Zell was sprinting.

Run, said an unfamiliar voice within James' being, taking hold of his soul with a powerful grip.

There was no time to think. Zell was a few seconds away. The urge to obey the voice overwhelmed James and tensed his body. He spun and bolted toward the edge of his instincts.

I trust you.

James vaulted forward. The cliff's edge passed beneath his feet. He heard Zell's feet slide and stop. He felt his new enemy's hand swipe at the back of his shirt and find no hold. James belonged to the air.

He squinted as a blue and orange flash skimmed the surface of an invisible bridge before him. His foot fell with a thunk, then a second step and a third. His stride was never interrupted. He looked down and yelped at the black void below. His eyes told him he was running on air, but the sound of heavy wood boomed beneath him and vibrated through his body. The water he couldn't see roared louder. Then new terrain shot into view: another cliff, a steep bank, and the edge of a river rushing a tree's height beneath his feet.

Jump, thundered the voice within him.

A blue and orange gleam lit the end of the bridge and drew his eyes. With another low yell, James left his feet and leaned back into a free fall. He gripped the map tightly. The water zoomed toward his falling frame.

Here we go.

He plunged into cold, swirling depths like an anchor, sinking deeper. Relief washed over him as quickly as the rushing water. He slowed and stopped. He opened his eyes. James hovered under and over the deep, suspended in a blissful embrace. Thousands of tiny bubbles kissed his skin. The chill overwhelmed but didn't jar him. The radiant particles that filled the air above filled the clear currents below. Some raced past him in obedience to the will of the river; some fell into the gravity of his presence and swept around him joyfully.

James held his breath but felt no urge to seek the surface. The floor was out of sight and the banks far away. Rays of light carved through waves overhead and shimmered blue and green. A refreshing river surrounded him, but James knew that something new and wonderful was at work within him.

The map regained his attention as it warmed in his hand. Its fiery light emerged again and drifted upward, unaffected by the water. James watched the smoke and fire wander away with the shimmering particles following and circling.

At last he gathered his strength and thrust himself toward the sky, his muscles aching from his tumble at the edge of the cliff.

After a few strokes, he burst into the air with a calm breath. The surface current spun him around, and there was Zell, little more than a speck standing far off on the cliff. He casually turned back and strolled into the woods. The river flow carried James downstream as he crammed the map into his pocket.

He drew a deep breath and tried to exhale the stress of their conflict. Beyond Zell's unnatural abilities, James couldn't make sense of the man's motives. Why was he so determined to keep him in that meadow?

His mind is as twisted as his tree.

It was difficult to regret leaving the path to follow Mary's voice, but choosing to follow the map from this point on was the easiest decision he had made in this new reality.

He turned to face the direction of the current. The banks eased farther away from each other—and from him—as he floated precisely between them. Though the sky still offered no source of light, the bright blue above had begun to shift yellow, patchy clouds drifting across the expanse like a crawling traffic jam.

There was no need to swim or tread as the river held him up and ushered him forward. The temptation to fight the flow to get to a bank was short-lived. A peace as deep as the river told him to wait and see what the waters willed, so he reclined and maintained his resolution to trust.

"I like this water better."

The river continued straight ahead but over the horizon. Though James faced forward, there was nothing to see except the scattered clouds that turned darker blue as the sky's deep yellow gave way to orange with unusual haste. He studied the changing colors closely. *When was the last time I actually watched a sunset?*

"Okay, so I've never watched a sunless sunset."

This world promised first-time experiences around every turn. He pictured Zell's glowing green eyes and decided not to ask for more surprises.

He looked right and left again to see that the rocky banks were now gone. Orange melted into the horizon, and blood red sprang up to take its place. The clouds zoomed away from the deepening crimson to join the riverbanks out of sight. So quickly the sky view shifted that James questioned his sense of time.

He swept himself around to look back. Nothing. James floated alone in a massive expanse of water. He looked down again, unable to pierce the deep darkness with his gaze. The once-clear view beneath had fled with the blue sky. He half-expected fear to work its way into his thoughts, but he found himself chuckling instead.

This river is safe. Hopefully, the same is true for where it leads.

He gazed straight up, and a few tiny stars claimed his attention.

"Where are you, Mary?"

Though the man he met in the clearing had given him reason to believe that she was alive—though he had urged James to find her—he couldn't imagine her in a safe place. He had to find her, whatever malevolent force had drawn her away. Whatever evil awaited him if he dared to seek her out. His aversion to conflict tested his mental resolve and was quickly squashed. He wouldn't abandon her to the force that had carried her into the darkness. Even if those wicked vines were conjured by his subconscious, he would help Mary—in any reality.

God, take me to her.

James hadn't realized that he'd begun to tread water while deep in thought. The current had left him still in a waveless ocean with a clear, dark gray sky watching from above, its million eyes sparkling brilliant white. His short history here had taught him to reach for the map when he didn't know what to do, so he lowered his hand to his pocket. A waxing glow from below the surface peeked into his peripheral vision, drawing his eyes down.

A hundred slithering ropes of orange light were already extending downward from his pocket, each reaching in a different direction below, each with a will of its own. They all searched beyond James' shallow depth of vision, twisting and rolling.

What are you doing now?

James looked up again as the sky reached the deepest black. The stars seemed either to move closer or grow larger by the second.

Suddenly a rush of water and a powerful splash thundered behind him. He whipped his head around to see a long wooden plank rocking on the surface—just in time to be shocked by another crash in front of him. *Splash! Splash!* Dozens of pieces of sunken wood shot into the air and clapped back down onto the water. James shielded his eyes from the unrelenting spray which now had a salty taste.

When the swishing and clattering ceased, he treaded at the center of a ring of jumbled wood of varying shape and size. James watched breathlessly as the orange tendrils surfaced and wrapped themselves around the wooden planks like the tentacles of an octopus. They dragged the pieces about noisily and carefully aligned board to board with perfect precision. Slowly the map remembered and regathered a vessel just as it was before breaking apart in the sea. A small boat un-sank before James eyes.

The orange glow illuminated and sealed every gap between the planks and stretched around, under, and across the boat. It rocked gently on the waves created by its assembly.

In moments, the swirling of the water and knocking and creaking of the boat-puzzle had settled and left only a mournful groan from below. James frowned and dipped underwater. The orange assembly network had spiraled around a thick mast, which was now rising toward the center of the boat, a sail wrapped around it several times.

He reached down to touch the energy emanating from his pocket and flinched when he was able to feel its physical substance, a warm web of pulsing strength. He narrowed his eyes and locked both hands around the collection of fiery cables that grasped the mast at the other end. With urgency he pulled himself along the strands, hand over hand, rushing to the vessel's approaching means of progress.

He looked up at the bottom of the boat. A hole remained for the mast to emerge through. He pulled closer. Stray fiery vines dragged a few more boards upward from beneath him. Finally, he joined the energy grasping the mast and glued himself to it with his arms and legs. Up he rose with the mast through the center of the boat, bursting into the atmosphere and rising toward the sky. He gained a fresh breath and held fast while the boards beneath him formed the boat's floor and attached the mast to complete the task at hand. The mast wobbled as the last piece snapped into place.

James looked down to find footing and dropped into his

new mode of transport, the weathered sail unfurling as soon as he landed. The glowing strands detached from the map in his pocket and joined the energy still gripping the mast. A flurry of orange zigged and zagged across the sail to stitch and patch every tear and hole in a dazzling light show.

The vessel was whole, held together by an unnatural force. Over his head and beneath his feet, a once defeated sailboat stood proudly on the sea, every part blanketed by a mesmerizing radiance.

James grinned and released a hearty laugh. The creaking planks seemed to join him.

"If I ever go back where I came from, I'm taking this map with me." He planted his fists on his hips. "I'd make a killing in construction—whoa!" The sail caught a gust of wind, and he was on his backside before he could admire his own joke. He rolled out flat and chuckled from his back. "I guess I'm not the only one with a fine sense of humor."

The boat hurried on without his consent, clearly on a mission. He scanned the width and breadth of the heavens that encased him and his transport, and then he focused past the familiar glittering air particles to fix his eyes on one star and then another. Each distant light above shined the same color but varied in size and shape—some oblong, some spiked, some giant and visibly rotating. At every moment at least a few shooting stars traced across the black canvas, curving in varying directions. The skies teemed with living light. The wind sang in his soul. The salty air invited him to breathe deeply.

James lay still and stared in awe for some time. He relished his tranquil stasis and made sure to move no muscle and savor the moment. Eventually the sound of the water breaking at the boat's stem set his mind in motion, and he followed his thoughts backward.

What happened back there?

In the midst of the bizarre events of the meadow and since, he said a lot of things he thought he'd never say.

"God, I blurted out that I believe in You. I called the name of Jesus for help. I asked You to save me. I told You I trust You." He shook his head. "What has happened to me?"

The plunge into the river filled his mind, and he could feel the chill overwhelm him again. A new feeling of joy competed with a swelling desire to confront his own nature.

"I spent so long running from everything that happened to Gloria. I didn't want that to be me. I didn't want my life to change. *I* didn't want to change. I just wanted to live my life the way I'd always planned." A tear joined a drop of sea water and slid over his temple. "You got in the way."

His dreams were long gone. The longing of his heart never saw the light of day. His idea of a fulfilled life was a bitter memory. Could there be something better? Could there be a greater purpose, a destiny that held a brighter future? A plan that meant more than happiness? A plan designed by God Himself?

He sat up straight. "My car was airborne, and You got in the way. I had no path through the woods, and You got in the way. I was under attack, and You got in the way." He stood awkwardly and grasped the mast. "I had nowhere to go but over a cliff into the darkness…"

He searched the symphony of stars for the right words before the wind closed his eyes. "I don't know where I am or if there's a way out. I don't know how to help my daughter. I don't know what's next." He wiped his cheeks with his sleeve. "I just know

I need You to be in the way."

Looking down, he pulled the map from his pocket and held it close to his chest. "It's pretty obvious that this map is part of the plan. It's been making paths and a lot more. So, *my* plan is to follow *this*, unless You say otherwise. Just keep leading. Keep speaking... I know I heard You."

He lowered the map and lowered his head. "I'm sorry it took me so long to listen."

Forgive me.

"Forgive me..."

James gasped at the sound of the voice he knew best.

"Gloria?"

"...and make me clean..." said the voice from overhead as it filled the sky and echoed over the waves.

James gazed up beyond the sail, his heart fluttering. The outline of his wife's face was set in motion by the host of stars above. They moved in sync to bring her back to life and turn the sky into a giant window to the past. Her lovely visage stretched across the dark expanse and replayed a moment James had seen with his own eyes twenty years prior.

"Be the Lord of my life..." Her head was bowed as she spoke softly. "...forever..."

"This is when she accepted Christ." James held back a sob and shook against the mast.

"...Amen." She looked up from her prayer and down at James and his boat.

"Gloria..." he whispered.

"James, I feel so different." She spoke through waves of emotion. "I've never felt love like this... I feel like... I'm not the same person anymore."

He remembered the words. He wanted to speak to her, but he knew that she wouldn't hear him. Instead, he stared and cried, unable to keep his heart from breaking again.

"James, everything just changed," she said with pure elation.

He wrapped his arm around his aching stomach and doubled over. He breathed in and out quickly to steady his mind and looked up again. The stars had returned to their places, having forgotten the picture they had just painted. Gloria was gone again.

James collapsed to the floor of the boat and succumbed to his anguish. It was the happiest he had ever seen her, and he had despised the moment with all his heart. He had hated the change in her, and she had loved that change more than her own life. New love, joy, and peace had filled her, and James would have stolen it from her if he could.

Now, though—now he understood. Now he longed to tell her that he believed. She might have treasured that moment over the moment he'd just relived in the stars.

God, I miss her.

James lay on his side. He tried and failed to recall his response to her profession of faith. He had spent years trying to forget the birth of the belief that had changed their relationship. His eyes drooped, and he yawned. Fatigue washed over his body, and he let his eyelids fall shut.

He raised them again and immediately closed them tightly to keep out a blinding light. He wriggled and found warm sand shifting under his arms and neck. Gulls called from the sky. He forced his eyes open. Gentle waves rolled over a golden beach. As his pupils adjusted, he spotted his boat's sail crumpled in the sand far off.

He rolled onto his back and started. A little girl with wavy, brown hair stood over him. A lump sprang to his throat, and tears flooded his eyes.

"Mary?"

SIX

"How do you know my name?" Mary whipped a short, wooden spear in front of her and held its sharp point an inch from James' nose.

James could do no more than lie speechless with his face soaked, staring at the visage of his little girl. Mary stood over him exactly as she had been at eight years old. She had begged for this haircut before she started the third grade.

Mary kicked his thigh. "I asked you a question."

Confusion crawled over James' features. "It's me, Mary."

"Well, 'Me,' is that the only name you have?"

"I…"

"So, do you prefer to go by 'I' or 'Me'? Because I want you to feel at home on my island, especially since I didn't invite you."

James begged with his eyes to be recognized, but Mary kept him pinned to the sand—more with her icy glare than the tip of her spear.

"Mary, I'm—"

"We've established *my* name, which I already know. Now I

want to know how *you* know it."

James blinked furiously. "I think... I need a moment." He closed his eyes again.

What is this?

James recoiled as Mary spiked her spear into the sand beside her.

"Well, I'm pretty sure you aren't here to do me any harm." She looked down and then back up his sprawled frame. "You don't even have *yourself* together."

After a moment of silence, James sat up with a grunt and lifted his gaze slowly up to her sparkling amber eyes.

It's really her.

She folded her arms. "How did you get here?"

James turned his head left and right. There was no sign of his boat, and no planks had joined him on the beach. He patted his clothes and found them dry. He would have suspected that he was dreaming on the boat if not for the sail on the sand not far away. He swept his right hand over his pocket and found the outline of the map. "I don't know," he sighed. "I was on a boat. And... now I'm not."

Mary's melodic laugh filled his ears and broke his heart. He smiled as another tear rolled down his cheek. He couldn't hold back his own belly laugh, and Mary laughed harder.

James looked into her eyes. "I can assure you that I have absolutely *no idea* what is going on right now."

Mary followed her meandering laugh to its conclusion at the end of her breath and sighed like a good laugh had filled her soul.

"If I told you how I know your name..." James watched her smile vanish. "You would never believe me."

She dropped her shoulders.

"I'm beginning to think I might be a crazy old man."

She grinned with a skeptical brow. "Well, then, crazy old man... What's *your* name?"

"James."

Mary looked off as if searching for his name somewhere in her memory. She snatched her spear from the sand, spun toward the palms behind her, and called out over her shoulder as she marched off. "Let's take care of that elbow, James."

He looked down at his right arm and found a stream of blood crawling away from a small scrape. "Huh. I guess I can still bleed."

He peeled himself from the beach and awkwardly lurched behind her, trying to keep up. He studied her purple shorts and white T-shirt, which looked like play clothes he had seen before. The sand hardened as she led him around scattered palms and bushes and through the opening of a small trail. Palm and palmetto leaves lined the floor beneath them, flattened paper thin.

They stepped over fallen trees. He swatted through branches, while she scurried around them. The path wove around towering old palms, careful not to encroach on their already claimed space. Brightly plumed birds hopped and flitted throughout the patchy canopy above them. Their chatter grew louder and more spirited the deeper James and Mary trekked into the wild of the island. James massaged his neck after he noticed that he hadn't stopped shaking his head since he stood up on the beach.

Mary juked right off the trail, dropped her spear, and scampered up a short palm tree with incredible ease. James gawked upward as she twisted two coconuts loose and sent them plunking to the ground. After sliding back down as quickly as she had ascended, she scooped up one coconut and smacked it into James' chest before leading on with the other under one arm.

The path narrowed and widened as the palms willed, their fronds offering more shade as they went. A gathering of fluorescent green birds made a game of following them directly overhead while ducking in and out of the surrounding branches.

James grasped one of the many thoughts that swirled through his mind like a school of fish. "How long have you been here?"

She paid him no attention but darted to the right through a small grove of papaya trees; she skipped and swung around the trees in a pattern more suited for enjoyment than efficiency. James followed quietly in a straighter line. Beyond the trees a new path turned from packed sand to granite and stepped down like haphazard shingles. Rough brown and gray rock climbed skyward on the right and left in spiking waves. The pair passed a shallow but wide spring on the right, which interrupted the ascending rock, with palms bending over its edge like children peering into a wishing well.

As the path descended, the rock walls swung wide and high and curved to meet in the middle and end the walkway with a towering cliff. A jagged opening was carved straight ahead in the rock face, but the path dove downward before reaching the elevated cave. Lengthy bamboo, cut neatly and bound together tightly with vines, formed a broad bridge leading from the plummeting path to the cave's entrance and invited them inside.

Mary galloped over the bridge and into the cave. James paused and took a few steps back to the glistening spring. He stood for a moment and watched tiny, golden fish zip here and there just below the surface. After rolling up his sleeves, he got on his hands and knees at the water's edge. He stretched his left leg far behind himself as a counterweight and leaned over to scoop a drink with his hands. Mary grabbed his foot and cleared her throat to stop his awkward effort and then swung low to dip a drink for him. She handed him a white plastic teacup full of cold water and bounded back into the cave. James sat up on the rocky path, dumbfounded, staring at a teacup from the set that Gloria had bought Mary while she was still a baby.

"There's no way."

His heart had not stopped aching since the island dream had begun. At the same time, he wanted to disappear from this eerie situation and gather little Mary in his arms and weep over her. How could the map lead him from the peace of the river to this unsettling place?

Why is this happening?

James willed himself to his feet. His walk over the bridge was less than graceful. He found Mary breaking down a coconut on a sharp rock when he entered the cave. Opposite the entrance sat Mary's childhood bed, a wooden frame with ivory headboard and footboard. It held up the same mattress, her favorite lumpy pillow, and her pink sheets. The stuffed bear and unicorn that had watched over her since her struggle with fear of the dark sat in their rightful places. Her nightstand, her dresser, her toys—everything but the walls was here. The scene was plucked from a different time and pasted into a place it didn't belong—a place that offered no warmth or comfort.

James rubbed his eyes, still unable to believe them. A large collection of framed pictures was somehow attached to the cave walls. As he stepped farther in to look closely, she pulled his attention away by placing a large piece of coconut meat in his free hand.

"I don't know."

"What?" James was still dazed.

"I don't know how long I've been here." She smashed the other coconut with intensity. "As long as I can remember. And that's a long time."

"How did you get all these things here?"

"What do you mean? This is my stuff. It's always been here." Mary didn't bother looking at him.

"In this cave?"

"You mean my room?" She gave him a look that dared him to offend her.

"Your room." He took a bite and tiptoed toward the photos with a swelling apprehension. Her first soccer game, her second-grade spelling bee victory, birthdays, Christmases, summer vacations. Meaningful moments covered the walls, dozens of frames that looked familiar. He scanned them frantically. He knew these photos. But they were different. He wasn't in them. He spotted Gloria over and over, holding her, laughing with her. He was nowhere to be found. Even in family photos where he had once been, there was space for him in the shot but no one there, like Gloria and Mary had a photo shoot with a ghost.

He turned his back to her to hide more tears and try to keep himself from sobbing aloud.

He had to force the question through his constricted throat. "These pictures..." His voice wavered. "Where is your dad?"

"That's a little personal," Mary said casually. She slid to his side and began to clean his scrape with a cloth. "If you must know, he wasn't really around. My mom talked about him a lot, but I don't remember him. Sad stuff, I know." She wrapped another cloth around his arm and tied it.

James tightened every muscle in his frame to keep from trembling.

"It was my mom who was really there. She was my whole world."

James didn't want to ask, but he couldn't stop himself. "Was?" His voice cracked.

"Yeah, she died years ago."

A wave of nausea overcame him. Beads of sweat speckled his forehead.

I can't do this.

"I'm so sorry for your loss," James squeaked. He held his breath and strolled to the cave's opening. He tottered over the bridge and released his composure at the edge of the spring, falling to his knees and heaving silently over the water.

"God, what is this place?" He kept his voice low and let his tears disappear into the pristine spring.

Then he saw it. *My reflection.* His mind raced back to the lake in the meadow, the water that didn't move, the glass surface that was willing to reflect everything but him.

Zell said that lake was pure peace. But it wouldn't tell the truth. He drew a deep breath. *The river moved me. And this spring is showing me who I really am.*

"I'm a failure." He lifted his head and clenched his fists. "I don't want to be a failure anymore."

What do I do?

Mary's voice broke the silence. "What's your deal?"

"Oh, I, um…" James wiped his face while he searched for an explanation.

"Having another moment, huh?" Her tone was blunt but held no hint of mockery.

"I guess I am... I'm not normally this emotional."

"Well, you're not having a very normal day. You hungry?"

Help her, said the gentle voice within his soul.

James relaxed his hands and shrugged. "I could eat." He pushed himself upright and followed his daughter back into the cave, two words echoing in his mind.

Help her... I don't know how.

She yanked open the creaky lid of her hope chest and gathered a variety of fruit in her arms. She dumped her findings on the miniature dining set that Gloria had purchased to take her tea parties to the next level. Mary squatted down on one of the rickety chairs that was far too small for her and began carving up chunks of papaya, guava, and starfruit with a wooden knife intended for pretend play.

"You really know what you're doing."

Mary swiveled her head, sending her wavy locks flying over her shoulder. "Why wouldn't I?" She went back to her chopping. "You know, it's kinda rude to talk to someone like they're a child."

James squinted. "Aren't you..."

She rose and swept past him to grab two plastic plates from her bookshelf. "Aren't I..." She used the knife to rake a serving of fruit onto each plate.

"You see that I'm quite a bit bigger than you, right?"

She handed him a plate. "I guess there's no shame in putting on a few pounds." She plopped onto her bed. "You do you."

Okay, I walked right into that.

James slowly took a bite as if trying not to scare away his train of thought. "Exactly how old *are* you, then?

Finally, Mary looked at him. "Indecent questions and

insulting comments. Kinda your thing, huh?"

James talked around a slice of starfruit. "I'm really sorry. I didn't mean to... I'm just really interested in your story."

"'Tell me your story' works just fine, crazy old man."

James raised a weak smile. "I'm sorry."

She waved her hand across the pictures on the wall. "I wish I had more recent photos. I don't know where they all went." She leaned over the footboard and collected a banana from the chest. "I was a teacher for a while. I decided it wasn't for me— or maybe the kids decided first. I was the *mean teacher.*" She only had one hand free for air quotes. "So, I got my master's in educational leadership. I turned out to be better suited for telling adults what to do."

Her banana became her classroom pointer. "Elementary principal for a while, then middle school, then high. Then I wound up getting my Ph.D. and teaching teachers in college. The farther I got from the kids, the happier I was. Not that I hate kids, right? It just wasn't for me."

It was all James could do to keep his expression from twisting into a knot. He couldn't reconcile the little girl before him with a woman far along her career path, especially as she sat on her childhood bed with her legs crossed. But he had no better idea than to play along. Mary seemed to be guarded, and he didn't want her to shut down. He knew that side of Mary too well.

"It doesn't sound like you have any kids of your own," he prodded.

"Not something I ever wanted, really."

"No husband?"

"Oh, you want the juicy stuff." She grinned and winked. "Nobody ever worked out. I was engaged once. I had my chances. But it was *always* my fault when things went south, of course."

"So, your dad—"

"Wasn't around, and I don't love talking about it."

James felt the sting of his own neglect. He paused for a moment before moving on. "And your mom…"

"My heart." Mary's smile seemed to bloom from roots deep in her soul. Her eyes danced in a way James hadn't seen in years. "She's the reason I believe in love at all. She made it real… every day. We had our differences, for sure. She was the most religious person I ever knew. That woman loved God and didn't care what anyone thought about it." Her eyes dropped to her bed. "I believed when I was a kid… I just saw things differently when I was old enough to question things. But she was *sincere*." A tear appeared on her cheek. "And she was *there*… That's what really mattered."

James smiled his approval of Gloria, but he longed for Mary to see him with the kind of love and reverence he had just heard.

"It's getting dark." She was leaning left and looking around him now. "The voices will be here soon."

"The…" James blinked away his thoughts and looked over his shoulder at the yellow glinting off the palm fronds around the spring. "Did you say 'voices'?"

"Unfortunately, we're not alone. I really wanted to be, but I can't shake the voices."

"You hear voices at night?"

"Boy, wouldn't it be great to just hear them?" she said flippantly.

"I'm sorry?" James leaned forward and dropped his hand to his knee to wait for the punchline.

Mary turned upside down and reached under her bed. "I know there's another one around here."

"Voices," James repeated, his eyes glazed over.

"Voices, James, yes." She dragged another pointy stick out onto the cave's cold floor. "Grab it. It'll help."

James squatted to pick up the spear with one eye squinted, muttering to himself.

"Oh, good. You like whispering. Everyone'll get along just great."

She swiped a teacup from her table and walked out to get herself a drink. James looked after her with a mixture of bewilderment and sadness swirling behind his gaze.

What has happened to you?

James pushed past his doubts. How a woman could appear as a child and tell him about a life not yet lived was beyond his grasp anyway. Real or imagined, James longed to understand how any future of his little girl could arrive at complete delusion. She had pushed her father out of her life and even out of her memory. And now her mother was gone. Was she so traumatized by Gloria's death that she had lost her mind?

Mary whisked back inside and wiggled a large blanket from the bottom drawer of her dresser. She flung it onto the floor along the entrance wall. "So sorry I can't do better. There used to be more to this house." She frowned at her bed and zoned out.

"Mary, why don't we leave?"

"We're on an island, James."

"We can leave the island." He tried to fill his voice with earnest compassion but failed to conceal his growing frustration.

"You were on a boat," she mocked. "And now you're not, remember?"

"I can figure out how to—"

She whipped around. "Look, I don't know you, and I don't trust you. If you'd like to vanish, fine. Everyone else does. *I* will not be leaving. *I'm. Fine.*" She held his gaze until a single tear had fallen from her chin to the stone beneath her feet.

"I'm so sorry, Mary." He softened his tone and spoke to her like he did when she was as young as she now appeared. "I have no right. I'm a guest in your home, and you've been a gracious host. You deserve more respect."

"Yeah, okay." She wiped her face and took his plate to the table.

James shuffled his feet and stared at the floor, hoping that he hadn't shut the door between them. "Hey, thanks for patching me up."

She took a deep breath and sighed. "Sure. I've gotten pretty good at binding my own wounds." She collected her spear from beside the dresser and sat on the edge of her bed. She stared out the entrance with her face fallen.

How do I help?

James sat on the blanket and rotated the spear in his hands. "So, the voices... What should I expect?"

She looked at him. "Probably nothing." She closed her eyes tightly. "No one else has ever heard them before—or felt them."

James contorted his face, afraid of where this was going. "So, what do they say?"

"It doesn't matter." She looked off.

"It matters to me."

"Look, I'm just hoping that you'll look scary enough to make them think twice about bothering me, okay? People help. Sometimes."

"Okay, Mary." Sadness consumed him. Empathy for her mental state ached through his being.

Mary rose and stepped toward the burgeoning night. "Sometimes I can kinda fight them off." She popped her knuckles. "Just... stay close, okay?"

"Hey." James waited for her to look at him. "I'm right here."

She nodded and faced the entrance.

Silence fell like a heavy blanket. Mary stared forward with her stance widened and countenance fierce. A soft breeze eased into the cave and swelled into a vicious gust that rattled the picture frames and sent her bedding into a wave. Silence and stillness prevailed again. Then distant labored breathing. Not Mary's. Not James'. Whispers were next—not like a secret, like a threat. A host of voices crept into the cave and echoed all around. Hollow shells of menacing gasps. Mary crouched lower. James stood and took his place behind her, his skin tingling.

A fine dust of orange and blue floated into James' peripheral vision. He shot his eyes downward and found the mist billowing from his pocket. Out of the cave it flowed on, ignoring the icy breeze that had started up again. James stared down at Mary and waited for her to acknowledge the unusual display, but she stood like stone. The mist spread forward, left, and right and formed a thin wall beyond the spring while the whispers grew louder.

A chill buckled James' back as a pitch-black figure emerged through the wall of dust and lurked toward them. Another. And another. A host of dark shadows shaped like starved old men lumbered forward with no eyes, gaping, toothless mouths, and their heads hanging far forward and wobbling at the end of long, frail necks. The shimmering dust lit their silhouettes and protruding jaws enough to reveal their sinister nature. They drew gnarled knuckles to the sides of their grave-like mouths to give direction to their malice.

Oh, God. James' courage wilted before he could attempt to hold it up.

Mary stepped onto the bridge and into the darkness. The unintelligible whispers crept closer. Over the spring the shadows glided; over the rock they trudged. Another gust of wind whistled through the cave, and James began to shudder as the temperature dropped.

"I'm warning you!" Mary screeched. "Get out of here!" She jerked her head in every direction, her icy breath blasting from her nose.

She can't see them.

"Mary, look out!"

The foremost shadow hovered onto the bridge with a withering breath and surged at Mary. She locked her eyes forward and lunged with her spear.

"Wait!"

Her thrust found its mark, and the creature scattered like smoke in a cloud of numberless particles. She shuffled backward. The bridge rattled. The shadow cloud whirled into a frenzy and reassembled itself into its original hideous form, marching on as it had before. Mary swung her spear wildly while James stood stunned, fixed to the floor. Mary backpedaled through the entrance at the moment a shadow reached into the opening from above and crawled into the cave on its ceiling, exhaling next to her ear. Mary dropped her spear with a shriek and scrambled to her bed, sobbing.

James let out a low yell and leaped at the figure overhead, slashing fiercely. He swiped again. The blows did nothing to impede the monstrosity. It floated to the floor, spinning upright, and lumbered on after Mary. James tried to wrap his arms around the voice and caught nothing but a piercing chill through his entire body. More shadows dragged into the cave, all of them laser-focused on the girl.

He stabbed. He swung. James stumbled backward and fell. Only one voice curiously craned its gangly neck toward him before turning again to its mark. They filed closer. Dozens were upon them. The cave filled with evil intent. Mary sobbed louder. James sat crippled by the cold. They slinked around the bed to form a perimeter and crouched over Mary.

Silence fell again. Only Mary's whimpering cry remained.

One by one each long neck reached forward like an outstretched arm to Mary's ear, and each gaping mouth delivered its woeful message.

"You're worthless."

"No one really likes you."

"Who would marry you?"

"You deserve to be alone."

"Your soul died with your mother."

"Your father never loved you."

Mary moaned as another shadow leaned in, and the voice that came from its mouth was the voice of James on the night of their last argument. His exact words growled into her ear. "Every desire, every dream, everything I have wanted I have sacrificed for your mother and for you… I didn't want this life…"

James sprung up, his pulse pounding. "Enough!" He loped to the bed's headboard. "They're lying!"

The whispers continued.

"You aren't who these voices say you are!"

Mary sobbed.

"This isn't you, Mary!"

"Stop yelling!" she wailed, clutching her knees.

James backed away. *This has to stop. God, make this stop!*

He snatched the map from his pocket and held it toward the shadows. In unison they turned toward James, still wheezing and murmuring. A brilliant flash of orange and blue bolted from the map like lightning and struck every creature's mouth with a loud crack. When the smoke of the strike cleared, the monsters' mouths were gone. Quiet. They groped their twisted fingers over their faces and necks in search of a voice, but silence would not be denied. One buckled and collapsed, then another. Each lost its strength, crumpling, writhing. And into the stone ground each faded out of sight, taking its frigid aura with it.

The air stilled. The cold withdrew. Mary lay shaking. James pocketed the map and rushed to her. He scooped her up into his arms and embraced her tightly as she cried.

It was his turn to whisper. "They're wrong, Mary. You're the most amazing person I've ever met. You're strong and kind. You're loving and loyal. You're a better person than I'll ever be." He wept over her.

"James."

"Yeah?"

She looked up at him with glistening eyes. "You heard them?"

"I heard them."

Her eyelids fell. "James?"

"Yeah?"

"I'm tired."

"Okay, Mary."

He laid her down gently on her side and covered her. With a

shaking hand he tucked her hair behind her ear and watched as the fear and anguish fled her small face.

SEVEN

James awakened to the sound of a coconut smashing against the sharp rock in the corner of the cave. Light rays danced around the spring's swaying palms and over the photo frames on the wall. Mary worked feverishly with her back turned to James. He stood and slid to the edge of the cave. He stooped to look up and around for a source of light and once again found nothing but shifting and swirling particles of visible atmosphere, always there to remind him that he was far from home.

The terror of the previous night lingered on his skin and threatened to send another chill through his body. He tried and failed to imagine what it would be like to spend every night suffering in such misery. Peace was what he held in highest regard, and little Mary's nights were filled with turmoil that no one could ever grow accustomed to without losing their mind. And now guilt pricked his heart after his assumption that she was mentally unstable. He scratched his head and searched for the right words.

Mary whirled around. "Drink this." She shoved a coconut into his chest with little tact and held her own coconut high over her head. The milk ran down both sides of her face. James couldn't hold back a smile.

He took a drink and stared down at her dripping chin. "You got a little…" He nodded toward her messy face.

"Who do I need to impress?" She wiped her chin on her shoulder. "You?"

James chuckled. "I'm already impressed." He flourished the coconut. "I'm not sure I'd know what to do with one of these."

"Well, if you're gonna stay, you're gonna have to learn." She returned to the table and began hacking at her husk with the wooden knife.

James frowned. "Mary, I can't—"

"You heard them… No one has ever heard them before. I've told family, friends, boyfriends, concerned citizens… No one has understood. No one gets it." She spun in her chair. "*You* actually heard them."

He dropped his gaze to his feet. "I've heard voices like that before."

"Voices have terrorized you before?" True curiosity colored her tone.

"Well…" He thought back to the nightmare they had just weathered and shook his head. "Something like that."

Mary waited for him to continue.

"I used to believe some things like… like what they said." Pain tightened his features as he looked up at her. "I've never thought much of myself."

Mary cocked her head to encourage him on.

"My dad didn't think much of me. And he would say things that a parent should never say. I would hear his voice in my head all the time. And eventually… I didn't need to hear his voice anymore. I got really good at saying those things to myself."

Mary scrunched her face. "Why would you do that to yourself?"

James thought for a moment. "I guess it was easier to believe him than it was to prove him wrong."

Mary turned back to the task at hand. "Well... That's dumb."

James grinned. He had no rebuttal. "Yeah, I guess it is."

His face fell again. His heart ached. He longed to make things right.

What have I done to her? He looked at the wall filled with pictures. *I couldn't get my father out of my head...* He focused on a family photo with an empty space where he once was. *She can't even find me in hers.*

Mary rose, walked to the corner, and broke her coconut in half on the rock. "So do you have a family?"

The question snatched James' attention, but he struggled to find a response.

"You know... Wife? Kids? Fur babies? I'm seeing the whole picket-fence vibe with you." She turned her head to him and flashed a facetious grin. "You look like you make good money."

He returned her smile. "That's funny." He looked at the floor and nudged a pebble with his foot. "I, um... My wife passed away."

"I'm sorry."

"And I actually have a daughter." He swallowed the lump in his throat. "She's nineteen, and, uh... our relationship isn't so great right now."

"What's her deal? You've gotta be a great dad."

He looked up through tears. "No, I really haven't been a great dad at all." He whistled out his hesitation. "I'm beginning to realize that my daughter needed more from me. I was there, but I really failed to be present in the moment." He directed his confession to the little girl in front of him. "She needed my voice in her life, and it just wasn't there."

She frowned at him with her mouth full of coconut meat. "Well, have you tried apologizing?"

He smiled broadly. "I *really* want to try. But I have to find her first."

Little Mary wriggled with excitement. "Ooh! Drama! *Intrigue!* Find her, you say? She's missing? Hiding? Tell me more, crazy old man." She giggled and dove under her bed. Toys and shoes skittered and rolled out onto the cave floor. She emerged with a grunt behind a pink backpack. James looked down at her sideways as she brushed herself off, zipped open the bag, and flung open a dresser drawer. "But tell me on the way."

"On the way?"

She spun and grabbed his arms. "We're going to find your missing daughter."

"*We...* are?"

"James, no offense, but you're not very resourceful. Life is a lot harder than coconuts, and—trust me—you could use some help."

James searched the rocky ceiling for a reason not to attach her to his mission. All he found was another chuckle.

God, what do I do? He remembered the voice within him. *Help her.*

"It could be dangerous," he teased.

"My middle name."

I happen to know it's Frances.

James shrugged dramatically. "Okay."

"Okay."

"Okay, *but*—"

"But?"

"*But!*" He belly-laughed. "You've got to ease up on the sass."

She gasped. "I'm sorry, did you say *saaass?*" She cackled and leaned into him.

"Sass, Mary. This crazy, old man can't keep up." He put his arms around her, and she squeezed him around the waist. "If I wouldn't let my daughter talk to me like that, I sure won't let you do it, ma'am."

"Fair enough." She tore herself away and resumed her packing. "We've got work to do, good sir."

"Work, huh?"

"Work, James." She slammed a drawer and looked at him with a playful smile. "We're on an island. And I don't have a boat either."

James clapped his hands together. "This'll be new."

* * *

James and Mary walked side by side along the beach where she had found him unconscious. The waves rolled onto the sand and left sparkling shells of distinct shapes and colors with every ebb. The cloudless sky served as a playground for gulls and tropical birds, their calls competing with the tumbling of the tide. Flashes of green, yellow, and red pulled James' head from left to right and back. Mary made a game of kicking the white sea foam when it crossed her path.

James took a loud breath of salty air. "Now *this* was convenient." They slowed and stood over the crumpled sail covered in seaweed. "This is a whole lot better than Plan B."

"Plan B?"

"Your bed sheets."

She punched his arm. "You leave my stuff alone."

A small, spiraled shell on top of the sail jittered, and long armored legs peaked from underneath. James watched closely as two stalked eyes slipped out and up, one focusing on Mary and one on James.

"You don't want to try to eat those," Mary said without a hint of jest.

"You tried—"

"Don't ask." Mary turned back.

"Don't ask, right," he repeated to himself.

They stretched out the sail on the sand and picked it clean of debris before folding it carefully. As they strolled back toward the path, they kicked the shallow waves up at each other. Laughter and banter filled the air and filled James' heart. When they reached the trail back to the cave, James pretended to struggle with the sail and let Mary walk a few steps in front of him.

"My daughter is going to help me find my daughter," He muttered quietly. "My little girl looking for my grown girl. My *older* girl, who actually looks like my *little* girl… My *future* girl, who looks like my *past* girl, looking for my *present* girl…" He nodded a few dozen times. "Yep. Okay, God. Got it. Good stuff. Good talk."

He glanced down at his pocket and found that the map offered no guidance. His heart told him that Mary needed to leave this island as much as he did.

It only makes sense not to go back the way I came.

They followed the trail past the cave and over a stream fed by the spring. The trail ended and forced them to weave through trees and plod through brush. They trekked toward the sound of the waves on the other side of the island. James struggled in earnest to bring the sail through the island's vegetation, holding it overhead, left, right, and walking backward through denser areas with sturdier branches. Mary buzzed around James like a bee, playfully wandering ahead and accepting every low-hanging branch as an invitation for a swing. The trees thinned as the ocean grew louder.

The beach on this side was almost identical to the other. An indecisive wind tossed Mary's hair in every direction. The shell creatures here were more active and seemed to like sparring with each other. A short cliff bordered the sand to the right, not far from the opening where they emerged.

James whooped and broke into a goofy dance on the shore. "Oh, yeah! Oh, yeah!"

"Ew, stop! I'm gonna hurl!" Mary wrapped her arms around him. "I can't let you do this to yourself!"

"You didn't tell me about *this*." He pointed above the cliff. A bamboo forest stood proudly against the bright blue sky.

"Bamboo, huh?"

"Bamboo, baby!"

She stretched backward and yawned. "So that's the big idea?"

"Mary, you know coconuts. But *I've* watched a lot of movies." He stared up at the forest with his hands on his hips and a twinkle in his eye. "I knew it would eventually pay off."

"Maybe it'll work. But those dance moves will never pay off." She hooked his arm and looked up at him with feigned concern. "Someone married you?"

James narrowed his eyes at her. "Watch it." He gave her a stone-faced wink and looked back up. "This is gonna be fun."

James led the way around the backside of the cliff through a crowd of swaying palms. The steep hill teased them with a slanted bed of fallen fronds that slipped under their feet. James' breath was spent far before he reached the bamboo.

"Is now a good time for a piggyback ride?" Mary asked.

"Yeah, I think I can only carry myself right now." James bent with his hand against a palm.

"I meant you."

James trudged upward with a series of grunts and groans and turned when he noticed that Mary had stopped.

She frowned at him. "You know, if you don't appreciate my jokes, I try harder."

"If you try harder, you'll explode."

"What a way to go!" she belted.

The closer they drew to the towering bamboo, the more James scratched his head, and the lower his eyebrows sank.

"Uh, oh. You looked a lot more confident on the beach when you were breaking all the rules of dance."

"It's fine." James grasped the first bamboo stalk they reached and looked it up and down. The stalks were thick, green, and sturdy. He pressed his weight against it and sighed. "This is bigger than I thought." He walked the perimeter of the grove with Mary at his heels. His head didn't stop shaking until he reached the other side. "Is this it?"

"This is it, chief."

James slipped into a trance, occasionally lifting and then immediately dropping a finger with an idea that had fallen apart as soon as it had arrived.

"So which movie is coming in handy?"

James twisted his face into a caricature and faced Mary. "This would be a lot more fun with tools. You wouldn't happen to have a saw under your bed?"

She raised one eyebrow.

"An axe?"

"Nope."

"A knife that isn't wooden?"

"Nuh-uh."

"A rusty sword?"

Mary laughed. "I do have an ancient golden lamp with a genie inside. I think he mentioned something about making all of my wildest dreams come true. Nice guy, actually."

Of course! "Ha-ha, smartie pants," James said coolly. "Could you look around for a sharp rock?"

James pretended to inspect the nearest stalk until she was out of sight. "Come on, come on…" He squeezed his hand into his pocket and withdrew the map. "*Please, please* do this for me. I need a break." He looked over his shoulders for Mary and unfolded the map quietly. The ink gave no hint of supernatural radiance; it stared back at him, black and cold. He extended his arms in front of his chest. "God, please cut the bamboo down." He closed one eye, waited a few seconds, and leaned his head close to the map. "Can you, uh… blast a few stalks over?" he whispered. He closed his other eye and leaned his head back. "How 'bout a magical hacksaw made of fire?"

He jumped at Mary's footsteps and scrunched the map into a wad before hunching over and apologetically folding it properly and smoothing it out.

"How about this, boogie man?"

He straightened and slipped the map into his pocket with his arm pinned to his side as he turned around.

"Oh…" He looked down at a smooth, clam-shaped stone with a blue-green hue and a sharp edge around most of its circumference.

Mary made no effort to hide how proud she was of her find. "Not bad if you do say so yourself right now, please."

"Not bad at all, Mary." He accepted the stone and tested its weight in his hand. "I'm guessing you don't have a good pair of work gloves."

She didn't bother to respond.

James tiptoed around the grove to the first stalk that bordered the rock face. He crouched and made sure that Mary was out of his range. *Here goes nothing.* He found a comfortable grip on the stone with his right hand and stretched his arm behind his back. With a grimace he swung for the lowest internode. The stone bounced off the bamboo and flew out of his hand and over the rock face. Down it plummeted to the sand below.

James stood straight up and massaged his palm before leaning on a stalk beside him. He scrunched his nose and waited for Mary's inevitable remark.

"James."

"Go ahead."

"No, you've got a hitchhiker."

He looked at his shoulder and locked eyes with a small shell creature. It must have sensed danger, because it scurried sideways down James' arm, over his hand, and onto a bamboo branch.

James jumped. "Mary!"

"What?"

The bridge!"

"The bridge?"

The bridge to your cave!"

The bridge to my room?" She shot him a glare.

He spun and grabbed her shoulders. "What is that bridge made of, Mary?"

"Aah, there it is."

EIGHT

Mary took a final look in her backpack and zipped it shut. She stood up and glanced to every corner of the cave, as if she wanted to carefully seal the moment in her mind.

James rested a hand on her shoulder. "Are you sure you have everything you want?"

She spun around. "I'm good," she called as she skipped across the bridge.

James waited until she bent to dip some water from the spring before stepping quietly to the wall and grabbing the picture frame that he found most haunting. It released from the cave wall with a click, and when James inspected the wall and the back of the frame for an explanation of its mounting, he found no answer. He slid the family photo out of the frame and stared at the space where he should be; he wished himself into that void and into her heart.

Mary had packed no photos. She simply said that her mother would live in her mind and heart forever. How had James disappeared from both so completely? He laid the frame on her now-bare bed, folded the photo, and slipped it into his chest pocket before fastening the button.

He stepped gingerly over the bridge. "Ready? Last chance."

"Do it, boss."

He squatted low and used the clam-shaped stone to cut the vines holding the bridge together. James and Mary helped the stalks separate and fall over the edge of the cave's entrance. The chatter of the birds paused while the bamboo clonked against the bottom of the path about eight feet below the cave floor.

James reviewed the hypothetical construction of the raft in his mind over and over while he dragged the bamboo trunks one by one to the shore. Mary gathered vines to bind the raft together. With a few breaks to eat and rest, the day was almost gone when they had gathered their materials on the beach and woven many of the vines into ropes.

James lay on the spread-out sail, barely able to move. Mary sat beside him with a banana in hand. The stars glittered as they peaked through the fading gold above.

"What are we gonna find on the other side of the sea?" Mary said.

James watched the ocean breeze tease her hair while she studied the horizon. "One thing I've learned in life is that you never know what's coming."

"What if I told you I've never left this place before?"

James sat up. Every muscle in his body protested.

"I've had lots of chances… but I could never bring myself to leave. People have tried. People that really did care about me." A tear traced her jawline. "They wanted to help me break free… to move on with my life. But every single one of them… I let them walk out of my life. *Sail* out of my life, actually."

She looked at James with red eyes. "Why did I choose this

place over love... over friendship?" With each word more anguish filled her voice. "I could have been happy."

James searched her eyes for hope. "I think... when you don't realize how important you are to other people, it's easy to write yourself out of your own story... to stop moving forward."

Mary looked down.

James touched her arm. "I don't know what's coming, but I'm learning that it takes a leap of faith to really live. A leap of faith is what got me here, actually. And if anyone in the *world* was made to live... I'm looking at her right now." He lifted her chin. "Mary, you have so much more to offer than you know."

* * *

James woke first. The smell of the ocean lifted him onto his feet. For a few moments He smiled over Mary who was wrapped in the sail like a burrito and purring like a cat as she slept. He padded to the sea and let the tide bathe his feet in cool water—the best substitute for a morning cup of coffee available.

If I'm gonna help her get off this island, I'm gonna need You to help me.

He allowed the clunking together of the bamboo stalks to serve as a wakeup call for Mary as he aligned the hollow pontoons into the large rectangle that had served as Mary's welcome mat at the cave. She stirred and gathered a breakfast of fruit while he wove ropes around the bamboo and the fallen branches he had laid across the raft. After working together to bind the base of their vessel, they turned their attention to making a mast out of a large branch with cross beams to support the sail. Mary wove more vines together into ropes to secure the cross beams and give them guides for the sail. She teased James throughout the process of attaching the sail to the mast—a process that pushed his patience to its limit.

James guessed aloud that it was late in the afternoon as they shoved the raft into the shallows, based on the color of the light around them. Warmth from no particular direction baked his neck. He had to dig his feet deep into the sand to move the raft a few inches at a time to the water. Once the vessel was afloat, Mary held it steady with a rope while James boarded the raft to test its buoyancy and make sure that the mast would rise properly when the time came. Finally, James' turn came to hold onto the raft while Mary retrieved her backpack and climbed aboard.

James walked the raft into deeper waters. "Ready?"

Mary's smile beamed with enthusiasm.

James whispered a prayer of thanks for the small stature of the waves that advanced on the island. *That's always the hard part in the movies. Building this raft was hard enough.*

He pushed until the water was chest deep and climbed aboard to lift the mast. "The wind is blowing pretty strong in the right direction. I'll take it as a sign that we're going the right way. You might want to hold on to something."

Mary lay low and grasped a branch with the tips of her fingers. "Give her the gas, cap'n!"

James heaved up the mast and guided the base down into a gap he had reserved for the middle of the bamboo lineup. A perpendicular branch fixed to the bamboo kept the mast from falling back down.

As soon as the mast was secure, the sail was full, and they

quickly gained speed, easing over a series of small waves. The raft moved briskly away from the island without veering left or right. James decided that the wind and waves obeyed a higher power, and he tied off the guide ropes. A couple of gulls flanked them with much to say about their departure. No swells appeared between the raft and the horizon.

James exhaled. "Nice view, huh?"

Mary sat with her legs crossed, facing the island. The wind blew her hair over her face and hid her expression.

"You okay?"

When Mary didn't answer, James decided to give her a moment. He busied himself by putting his shoes back on and crawling around to inspect the base of the mast and check the integrity of every vine-wrapped joint on the raft.

When he ran out of tasks to fill the quiet between them, he paused to consider the gravity of her decision to leave behind all she had ever known—and leave it via the ocean on a raft made by someone with no raft-building or seafaring experience. He searched his thoughts and decided to compare her commitment to flying for the first time on a one-way trip away from home forever, with a captain who had never even seen a cockpit.

When too much awkward silence had passed for James' patience, the island was almost gone. He scanned the breadth of the horizon for land and found none. The gulls turned back and called their goodbyes. Grey tones invaded the blue above.

James steadied himself behind Mary and cupped her shoulder. She immediately shrugged him off.

"Mary?"

She dropped her head, and James started to scoot backward. He stopped himself and shook his head. *I got into this mess by backing up.*

"I'm here when you want to talk."

James lifted his eyes up to pray, but he hung his mouth open instead. A pinwheel of dark clouds spun straight over the raft. He gazed upward as it grew with unsettling speed. The farther the large, gray lobes stretched, the wider they spread. The blues above seemed to melt away. The clouds began to growl. Mary sat silent and still.

When the sea beneath the raft began to swell, James decided it was time for conversation. "Mary, are you good?"

She was quivering now. He leaned around her and pulled back her wavy hair. Mary's face was soaked with tears, her eyes thin, her brows sunk. "I'm so sorry."

"Mary, what—"

A deafening rumble sent the clouds spiraling faster. The canopy thickened. More dark gray spilled and scattered downward, rushing closer to the sea. The raft lifted and fell far enough for James to instinctively gather Mary into his arms.

She whimpered. "I can't."

"We're gonna be fine. Let's just lower this—"

A piercing gust snatched the sail and snapped a rope. James and Mary rolled onto their sides. The raft careened over the side of a sizable wave and up the side of another. James groped for the broken rope, the mast shaking violently. *Pop, pop, pop,* the vines threading the sail around the lower cross beam broke and unraveled. The sail lifted and waved like a flag with the will of the wind.

"It's okay, Mary!" He held her tight with one arm and wrapped the other around the base of the mast. The swells swept the raft over higher hills and through lower valleys.

"I can't leave!"

"You already left, Mary! It's okay!"

"It's not okay!" she cried out, barely above the whistling wind. "You don't understand! I've tried to leave before! A lot of times!"

A wave of icy rain pelted their faces. The raft waltzed around the top of a massive swell and down its steep bank.

"Hold onto me!" James hollered.

Mary wriggled closer and clutched James around his chest. "Friends came, family came, people I wanted to love! I left with them, James! I got on their boats, but... I thought it would be different this time!"

James raised his voice over the storm. "This has happened before?"

"You're not the only one to wake up on the beach, wondering where your boat went... wondering where your life went... God, why do I do this?" She screamed as lightning flashed downward and blasted the mast. Sparks and splinters flew. The sail ripped away and soared up into the chaos. The top half of the mast gave way and disappeared into the depths.

"James!" She dug her fingernails into his back. "I'm not gonna make it this time! I won't come back this time! I'm gonna die!"

"Mary you're not going anywhere! *I'm* not going anywhere! I won't lose you again!"

"What?" she wailed.

"I let go of my daughter, and I'm not letting go of you!"

The vines holding the raft together popped and slithered around the bamboo like retreating snakes, tearing away from every joint. The pontoons inched away from each other.

"God, help us!" James shrieked into the din.

Out of his pocket a hundred orange tendrils whipped and wove their way around the raft's separating structure. James rolled Mary on top of his chest while the bamboo clunked into place. The stalks groaned their displeasure as the map's energy tightened around them.

The raft screamed down the side of the steepest wave yet and skimmed up the face of an enormous breaker. Higher and faster raced the raft until its nose pointed to the eye of the storm. James hugged the mast's base closer and sturdied his arm around Mary's backpack. He released a low yell. Mary released her grip.

"Mary, no!"

She slipped downward, looking into his eyes. "Thank you."

They soared over the edge and into the air, far above the surface below, the huge wave already rushing far away.

"You can't!" James' grip was too weak. Suddenly, she was airborne and flying toward the concrete, black ocean beneath. James didn't think. He spun and set his feet against the base of the mast.

"I love you!"

NINE

Launching with all his might, he dove into the downpour, leaping straight at Mary. He grabbed her in the air and rolled over in time to see a flash of orange and blue fire from his pocket and wrap around the broken mast.

They free-fell straight down. The map whipped the raft down through the turbulent air to scoop their bodies as another large swell rushed in to provide a ramp and a soft landing back on the surface. With lightning speed they careened down the wave, spinning wildly. James and Mary lay on the raft, eyes closed, bracing for the next wave, a wave that never came.

The raft spun and skied over the surface and slowed to a gentle float. They opened their eyes and looked up. The clouds circled overhead and vanished into their point of origin like water draining from a sink. With every second the atmosphere brightened, and the living particles around them seemed to come out of hiding and celebrate their survival. Dusk had fallen. The remaining waves rocked the raft like a baby, a sort of apology. Their heavy breathing emerged into James' hearing as the rumble of thunder and the roar of surf faded away.

"I don't understand." Mary rolled onto her back but kept her eyes where the eye of the storm had been. "What just happened?"

"You're still here." James gasped for air, his head wobbling. "That's what happened."

She sat up and looked down at him with wide eyes, shaking her head. "I gave up."

He sat up and held her gaze. "I wouldn't let you."

She dropped her head onto his chest and melted into his embrace. Her voice trembled. "Why? Why did you jump? You could've died."

He choked on the lump in his throat. "I'm trying, Mary... to make up for all the times I didn't jump for the people I loved."

"I'm glad you're here."

"Me, too, Mary."

James wiped the rain from his face and looked down at the bamboo under them. Around the joints, a glow of blue and orange pulsed, ensuring the craft would stay intact.

Time to talk then.

"Mary, so... the raft is still together. How about that?" he said sheepishly.

"Those movies definitely paid off. I'm honestly impressed."

"So, you don't... see anything different about it..."

"Well, now that you mention it, I see that the mast is destroyed and the sail is gone. When I called you 'captain,' I didn't mean 'Captain Obvious.'"

James smiled. "Mary's back."

So, she can't see this either.

"Hey! Look at that!"

James followed Mary's eyeline and squinted at the hazy

horizon. A tree line peaked through and spread wider as they floated on. James hadn't noticed the constant forward motion of the raft. He imagined a thousand tongues of fire paddling beneath them. He looked up at the emerging stars, twinkling, spinning, shooting.

"Just in time, too. We're gonna need a place to camp," James said.

Mary looked around with wrinkled brows. "So, what exactly is propelling us?"

James smirked. "I've learned to just go with it."

"Just go with it. Okay, fearless leader. I'm so glad to be alive right now, I'll let it slide."

They approached another sandy beach with little light left. Brilliant starlight helped them study the shoreline which hosted a wealth of large rocks and a mysterious feature straight ahead.

"Is that a dock?" Mary asked.

"I didn't expect to find a pier."

"You know a pier is a dock, right?" She looked at him sideways.

"Depends who you ask."

"Well, I'm not asking you, James. I already know."

James chuckled, and Mary punched his shoulder.

"I might kiss this dock-slash-pier." James gathered the longest rope still attached to what was left of the mast and leaned toward the approaching wooden structure.

Mary leaped onto the dock before James could finish tying the raft to a protruding post. She was darting around at the edge of the dark forest when James set foot on the sand.

"What are you doing?"

She shuffled away from the tree line and crouched over the

beach with her arms full of sticks. "We're back on my turf, big guy."

"What's that supposed to mean?"

"You're the boat guy. And the no-boat guy." She dug at a flat piece of wood with a small stone. "I'm the survival girl. And you need to grab some tinder."

"Do I look like the tinder guy?"

"You do if you want to have a lovely evening by a toasty fire. Chop, chop!"

"All right, all right." He turned to face the forest and looked right and left.

"There's some dry grass straight ahead, tinder guy," she said with a singsong tone.

James returned a couple of minutes later with two handfuls of dry grass and crouched beside Mary as wisps of smoke rose from beneath the round stick she was spinning furiously.

"Wow! That's amazing!"

"Quick! Put some right there… and give it some oxygen. *Easy.*"

James stacked some grass on the board, lowered his head to the ground, and gently blew. "Hey, Mary…"

"What?" She kept spinning.

"Are we having a… *tinder*… moment?"

She moaned. "Please stop. Don't stop blowing! Stop being such a dad. It's *physically* painful."

In seconds a flame appeared, and Mary dropped her stick.

"More sticks! Small ones. Go!" Mary barked.

A few minutes later they sat beside a roaring fire with a modest serving of fruit from Mary's backpack.

"You didn't tell me you could build a fire."

"You didn't ask."

He stared at her like he was truly seeing her for the first time. Had he lived in the same house with her for eighteen years and never known her? He thought of the laughter that often filled their home. It was always Gloria and Mary. They would sit and talk in Mary's room. They had inside jokes. Mary always wanted to be with her mother.

How could I have been so numb? She was right there all along. And I didn't really see her.

James said what he should have said many times before. "You really are an incredible person."

"Well, James, I can't say that you're wrong." She gave him an authentic smile. "But I can say, 'thanks.'"

Mary removed the clothes from her bag and laid them by the fire to dry. James rolled onto his back and closed his eyes.

Thank You… for this.

* * *

James and Mary awakened to the sound of sandpipers, calling to each other as if communicating by Morse code. They strutted by, unbothered by their visitors, probing the tide's edge for their breakfast. The once raging fire now offered nothing but a weak stream of wandering smoke. A thin fog stretched over the beach from the now mysterious ocean, barely distinguishable from the overcast, colorless sky.

Mary sat up and stretched high. "Banana?"

"Hit me."

She almost did. James caught the banana just before it smacked him between his eyes.

"Hey! It's too early for that."

"I've got a feeling you're gonna need sharp reflexes on this trip of ours." She busied herself by gathering her clothes and packing her backpack again.

James patted the clothes on his body and nodded as he found them dry. "Good thing we dried out. I don't suppose you have anything in that bag that would fit me."

Mary ignored him and marched toward the trees. James put on his socks and shoes and then bent carefully through his muscle soreness to stretch to his feet. He filled his lungs and blew the breath from his nostrils.

Here we go.

He stalked out of the thick sand to catch up with Mary, who seemed to be going on an adventure with or without James. He wondered how long it would take her to realize she was alone if he chose not to follow her.

"Eager, aren't we?" he called after her.

"Let's just say I'm ready to see something other than a beach!" She spun and walked backward a few steps to offer him a smile that seemed full of hope.

"So, are you planning to lead the way?" James moaned through a yawn.

"I'm just looking for *any* way."

"Fair enough," he said to himself.

James looked over his shoulder to make sure the raft was still tied to the dock and followed Mary along the coast, a proud line of huge gray boulders between them and the waves. A pleasant stroll later they found a broad path that welcomed them into the woods. Golden light emanated from within the forest as strong as the light that fought its way through the fog behind them. A blond glow outlined every leaf of the towering hardwoods on either side. Mary didn't hesitate to start down the path. James maintained his stride but glanced at his pocket. A toothy grin crawled across his face when he saw that orange and blue wisps of fire and smoke were drifting gently forward from the map.

"What's got you so excited?"

James almost ran into Mary. He hadn't seen her turn around. "Oh, I, uh… I'm just feeling optimistic. I really believe we're gonna find Ma—, my daughter."

He wanted to kick himself. *That was close.*

She hooked his arm and pulled him back into stride, walking beside him. "Of course we are. By yourself? Hmm, I gotta be honest with you. I didn't like your chances. Maybe forty percent? And those are generous odds. With me around, your success is basically guaranteed."

"I had no idea I was so fortunate." His grin returned.

The dirt path was hard and uninvaded by grass. Very few shrubs interrupted their view through hundreds of tall trees. Pines became more prevalent as they traveled deeper inland. Mary couldn't resist stopping at a wild grape vine, telling James she would've died for grapes on her island. He joined her for a snack. Hunger hadn't been a concern of his in this world, but he didn't want to raise more questions from little Mary. She stuffed her stomach and stuffed her backpack's front pocket for another round later.

The path veered slightly left and right but never changed direction quickly, and no alternate paths or clearings appeared for several miles. Mary seemed content to follow the path, with only one clear way forward. They filled the time with conversation about their serene surroundings, and after James' badgering, Mary finally told him about her attempt to eat one of the shell-dwelling creatures from her island. James laughed until his sides ached as much as his tired muscles. As the path stretched on, even Mary's pace became labored.

"Might be nice to have a seat for a m—" James froze with his head turned right, and his nerves sent needles over his skin.

Mary staggered to stay with James and then traced his intense stare through the woods. She spotted the house that held James' eyes like glue. "You all right?"

He walked off the path and followed his open mouth into the forest. "It can't," he said to no one.

"Need info, please." Mary stepped in front of him and walked backward.

James wouldn't look down at her. His eyes remain locked on the house while his head slowly shook right and left. "This is… This isn't…"

She rolled her eyes. "Well, that clears it up." She fell into stride beside him.

They approached a small house with cream-colored wooden siding and brown lattice covering a crawl space. A weathered porch with hunter green rails and steps led to a narrow door of the same color. One shutter was askew on the otherwise neat but aging home.

James halted when he saw a silhouette pass by a window, and his heart seemed to drop to his feet. He looked down at his pocket and sighed. The map's energy beckoned him toward the house.

"I don't know if I can do this," he muttered.

"Do what exactly? I think it's only fair to keep me in the loop here."

"Mary... This is my childhood home... This is my parents' house."

"Oh... Okay. Here?" She scratched her head. "That's not weird, right? That's weird. Is it?"

James massaged his temples. "It's pretty weird. But it's especially weird because it was torn down a few years ago."

Mary stood with her face contorted by confusion. "Does this fall into that 'just go with it' category?"

He walked on. "I think this is par for the course."

Mary followed. "I hate sports metaphors."

The nearer they drew, the louder the sound of TV news rose. Muted live voices mingled with those of the anchors—familiar voices. Blurrily the screen reflected in the left porch window. With every step, James felt heavier.

Mary grasped his hand before he set foot on the first step of the porch. "Wait."

He stared as if trying to see through the front door and took a deep breath. He said nothing but squeezed her hand to acknowledge her.

"Are you sure this is okay?"

He lowered his head and shoulders. "I don't know."

"I'm right here with you, big dog."

They looked at each other the moment the smell of fresh apple pie reached them.

"Welp." Mary bounded up the stairs and knocked on the door. "What's not to love about visiting your folks?"

Footsteps neared the door.

"Mary..."

"What?"
"They're dead."
The door opened.

TEN

A thin woman wearing a pleated green dress with her hair in a bun gazed at the back of Mary's head. The dread on Mary's face registered in James' mind, but he could only gawk at her until his mother cleared her throat. He forced his eyes up to Patricia's face, which appeared quite confused.

"James, honey, why are you knocking? And who's your friend?"

Mary tensed as Patricia touched her shoulder.

"Mom..." He could barely speak.

"James, *who* is your friend? Did you forget your manners, son?"

"This is—"

"Speak up, please." His mother nodded at him with a look that simultaneously encouraged and reproved him.

When he looked back down at Mary, her face was drawn into an uncomfortable pucker. "This is my friend Mary. Mary, this is my mother."

Patricia shook Mary's shoulder and startled her. "Hello, Mary! Are you new to the neighborhood?"

Mary darted her eyes around as if checking for any other homes and then landed them on James who was rapidly nodding. "Yes! I'm the... new girl?"

"She just moved here. Her family is from somewhere... else."

"Mary, it's a pleasure to meet you. Your timing is excellent. I *just* took a fresh pie out of the oven."

Mary's face relaxed. She craned her neck over her shoulder and looked into Patricia's eyes. "I suppose some pie would make things better." The last word sounded like a question. She peeked back at James, and he knew she needed his permission again to enter the house.

He forced a smile. "Pie sounds good."

Patricia strode into the house, and Mary padded behind her while keeping the corner of her right eye on James. He ascended the porch steps, and with each step his stomach turned more. As he crossed the threshold, he wobbled. The room spun. He closed his eyes and leaned left. The door jamb held him upright while he collected his balance.

What was that?

He pushed himself forward, through the foyer, past the dining room, and into the kitchen. He peered up at his mom, who was slicing the pie. He looked over at Mary, who gasped and slapped her hand over her mouth. The color drained from her face.

"J-James..." she whispered.

"What?" he hissed.

He looked up at Patricia and back down at Mary. Up at Patricia. Back down at Mary.

Oh, no... I'm shorter.

He lifted his hands in front of his face—small, smooth hands. He gasped and covered his mouth; only a faint wheeze was able to escape.

Patricia whisked past him into the dining room. "You can eat it in here. I'll get some ice cream. Do you like ice cream on your pie? James, loves it."

"Yes, ma'am." Her face and feet were frozen.

Patricia swept by again and took a carton of vanilla ice cream from the freezer. James stumbled through the kitchen, past his mother, and into the hallway. He closed his eyes as he passed the doorway to the living room and burst into the guest bathroom.

He turned on the light with a trembling finger and stretched onto his toes to see his fear confirmed, staring back at him in the mirror. He looked to be about the age of little Mary, as scrawny as he had ever been, and wearing his old favorite blue t-shirt.

When his eyes welled with tears, he smacked his cheek with his palm. "No!" he growled under his breath with a much higher pitch. "Keep it together, James." He pointed at his reflection. "*You* are *not* quitting now. Mary needs you. She needs a father who isn't in pieces. You can face whatever this place throws at you. *This* is just a part of the journey… an unexpected part."

He turned on the faucet and splashed some water onto his face. When he buried his face in the hand towel that hung on the wall, the smell of the laundry detergent dealt him another emotional blow.

"James…" Patricia's voice lilted from the kitchen.

"Just keep going," he whispered to himself. "Help me," he whispered to God.

He stepped back into the hall and tiptoed by the living room doorway. He glanced right. His father's recliner rocked gently, facing away from James. The glow from the TV lit the edges of the faded blue fabric. He glided through the kitchen and found

Mary eating apple pie a la mode while his mother toured her through a dusty photo album.

She turned a sticky page. "And this… was our summer beach vacation two years ago. James has always been afraid of the ocean. Look at that face!"

Mary giggled and winked at James. "Afraid of the ocean, huh? I'm glad I didn't know that. This pie is *so* good."

"Thank you, dear—James! Sit down! Eat your pie. Your ice cream is melting everywhere."

"Thanks, Mom." He sat and took a bite that sent a chill up his spine.

This is all too real.

"*So*, James, Mary tells me you met days ago. Why haven't you brought her over until now?"

James looked at Mary, who shrugged with her eyebrows. "She, uh… was a little shy about leaving her house. I didn't want to rush her."

"Well, Mary, you are welcome here *any time you want*. It's about time James had a friend who's not gonna get him into any trouble." She laughed at her own comment and walked through the kitchen and down the hall.

"*What* is going *on*, James?" Mary snarled with her eyes stretched wide. "This pie is *amazing*, but what in *heaven's name* is happening? Why are you a *kid?* What *is* this place?"

"I don't *know*," he whispered, holding his hands out to quiet her. "Shrinking wasn't on my to-do list." He paused to listen for footsteps and shook his head. "We'll just be nice for a bit, eat a little magic dessert… and then we'll slip out of here soon. It'll be fi–"

"James!" The deep voice of his father bellowed from the

living room.

James winced as his breath caught.

"You okay?" Mary spoke softly without moving her lips.

He held up his hand to reassure her, but his fingers trembled. His reply wavered. "Coming."

The floor howled as he pushed back his chair. He forced a steady gait through the kitchen and into the living room and presented himself just inside the peripheral vision of his father.

Robert's eyes seemed to go through the television set. His vacant look told a long, sad story that had always been a mystery to James. His thick mustache hid his emotion and muffled his words. "Son... did you not hear me when I asked you this morning to rake the yard?"

Terror filled James' heart. He didn't have the luxury of this recollection, but he had felt this dread many times before. "I, uh... don't remember. I'm sorry. I can do it no—"

"*If it wasn't already done...* maybe you could do that." He started at a roar and waned to a harsh rasp. "I'd like to know how I got blessed with a son who is apparently incapable of listening to me when I give him instructions and leaves me with *more* work after an *entire day* of back-breaking work to support this family."

"I didn't mean—"

"You didn't mean to what? Disrespect me? Disobey me?" Robert sat straight up and looked deep into James' eyes. "Disappoint me?"

James shivered under the power of his father's cold gaze. "I'm sorry, Dad."

"Do you know how *hard* I work, *Son?* Do you have *any* idea whatsoever how *exhausted* I am? Has it ever entered your mind how much of a *burden* I carry? Do you want to be a *part* of that burden, *Son?* Are you *trying* to make things worse?"

A tear formed on James' cheek.

"Oh, are you a *victim* now?" Robert probed his eyes as if evaluating his emotional weakness. "Is that how it works? You make things harder for everyone else and then you cry when they do your job for you?"

Robert reached out and gathered a handful of James' blue shirt before pulling him slowly within a few inches of his face. "James, I think it would be a really good idea for you to show some gratitude for what I did for you today. Some appreciation for what I sacrifice."

Two tears raced each other down James' cheeks. "Thank you, Daddy." He held back a sob with all his might.

Robert bared his teeth, and his voice reached its lowest growl yet. "You should probably get me a beer, boy." He slowly released his grip on James' shirt.

James walked back to the kitchen with as much composure as he could manage. He opened the refrigerator, and Mary startled him from behind.

"Are you okay?" she whispered. "Is your dad really that intense?"

James turned and frowned at her. "You shouldn't talk about him like that. He's my dad."

He reached into the refrigerator and collected a bottle of beer.

Mary stretched around him to meet his eyes. "I don't understand."

"I guess you don't." His face was empty of expression.

A thud drew James and Mary to the hallway door. Patricia was leaning against the wall, breathing quickly with heavy eyelids.

"Mom!" James dropped the beer bottle on the hall carpet and ran to his mother. "Are you okay?"

"I'm okay, James," she slurred. "I'm just feeling really tired, baby." She straightened herself and kissed the top of his head. "I'm just... gonna lay down for a little bit." She smiled down at him. "Thanks for looking out for me, buddy."

"James!" Robert barked. "Beer!"

James galloped back down the hall and scooped the beer on the way to his father. Mary stood in his way when he barreled back around the corner.

"James."

"What?" He made no attempt to hide his annoyance.

"What are you doing? Aren't we getting out of here?"

"What? My *mom* isn't feeling well. Something is wrong."

Mary pressed a palm against each wall when he tried to walk around her. James stepped back and gave her a scowl.

"Something *is* wrong... with *you*, James."

A shrill howl rang from the master bedroom. James bolted past Mary, almost knocking her down. He skidded to a stop at Patricia's side. She lay curled on her side in bed, clutching her abdomen. Beads of sweat speckled the side of her face.

"Mom? What's wrong?"

"Oh, it's nothing, baby. I just have a little stomach pain. It'll pass." She lifted her head to smile at him. "Could you, uh... get me the heating pad? I think it's in the living room."

"Okay, Mom."

Mary stood against the hallway wall and turned her head as James walked by on another mission. He walked into the living room with his eyes up and kicked over a cluster of beer bottles, sending a cacophony through the house.

"Hey! Boy!" Robert whipped his head around and looked at James with bloodshot eyes.

James scanned the floor. It was now covered with empty bottles. He braced for a scolding.

"Bring me a beer." Robert's tone was low and calm.

"Y-Yes, sir." James contorted his body to step over and around the mess. He swiped the heating pad from the couch and hurried back to his mother. Mary stood beside her and held a trash can while Patricia threw up into it.

"Mom!"

Patricia lay back down with her head in a wrap. Her face was thinner, her color faded.

"Mom?" Anguish filled James' voice.

Mary spoke softly over his shoulder. "James... this place isn't what it seems."

He turned and looked at her with a mixture of disdain and confusion. "Who are you?"

Mary's face fell. "James?"

"Get out of here! Can't you see my mom is sick? What are you *doing* here?"

"James, it's me!"

"Get out!" He walked her backward and slammed the door in her face.

When he turned back to his mother, she was even thinner, and her skin was yellowed.

"I need beer!" echoed down the hallway.

James started to run to his father but jerked himself back toward his mother to see that a small tube was delivering oxygen through her nose. Tanks were scattered throughout the room. She labored for shallow breaths with her eyes closed.

James trembled toward her.

"Beer!" A bottle broke and then another.

"Mom?" James wept, gasping for air.

"Hey, baby." Patricia managed only a whisper. "It's okay, honey. I'm just really tired." Her weight dropped before his eyes. The bones of her face and arms protruded.

James took her hand and sobbed.

"I... love you..." She gave his hand the slightest squeeze and released a long final breath.

"Beer! Get me a beer, you worthless piece of trash! Aren't you good for anything, or are you a complete waste of breath?"

James' heart groaned as he stared at his mother's closed eyes. His ears rang. His breath deepened and then accelerated. He laid down her hand and dug his fingernails into his palms. He marched to the bedroom door and flung it open, slamming it into the wall. "Why don't you get your own stupid beer?" he screamed down the hall. He waited for his father's response, blasting every breath out of his nose, the vein in his neck throbbing.

Robert stumbled into the hallway, barely able to stand. He leaned against the wall and forced his head level to look at James. "You know..." he rasped in a hushed tone. "Every time I look at you, I see her. And instead of feeling proud, I feel sick. I'm so sick that all I have left of that beautiful woman... is *you*."

James quivered. "You're drunk."

"James, I'm about as sober as I get these days... and I just want you to know something." He stared deep into his son's eyes. "I hate you."

James' tears flowed freely. "I don't have to listen to you." The strength had left his voice. He walked down the hall and tried to pass his father, but Robert grabbed his arm tightly.

"You don't walk away from me."

"Let go of me!"

"It looks like I need to teach you how to show some respect!"

James jerked away from him, but his father wouldn't release his grip. They wrestled in circles into the living room, and James reversed his pulling motion into a strong push. He sent Robert tumbling backward over a mountain of beer bottles, and he rolled behind the couch.

Silence. James could only hear his pulse thundering in his ear.

Robert chuckled softly behind the couch. "Look what I found."

James gawked as his father staggered to his feet and dragged little Mary upright by her arm. She whimpered with tears in her eyes.

"Maybe it'll get your attention if I teach *her* instead of you."

"James…"

ELEVEN

Mary.

The look in Mary's eyes snatched his mind back to reality. The gravity of the situation washed over him and swept away his confusion. Blind anger was replaced by unchallenged concern for his daughter. Robert tightened his grip, and Mary yelped. He steered her roughly to the middle of the living room.

What do I do?

James took a deep breath. "I'm sorry, Dad. I'll get you a beer right now."

Robert stared at him. Mary suppressed the sound of her rapid breathing. James walked into the kitchen and back into the living room with an unopened beer bottle.

As he approached his father, Robert relaxed his grip and released the tension in his shoulders. A smirk lifted his mustache. James narrowed his eyes at Mary before gritting his teeth and hurling the bottle with all his might at the space between them.

End over end the bottle flew and smashed into the TV screen. Glass cracked and splintered. Sparks flew. A loud zap preceded billowing smoke. Robert stumbled backward, losing his hold on Mary's arm. She fell forward onto the floor. Robert crashed into the lamp on the end table and fell on his back, bottles breaking beneath him.

James looked right to the back door and sprang toward Mary, slipping over bottles as he went. "Mary, let's go!" He pulled her to her feet.

"Why you little..." Robert inspected his bleeding left hand with sleepy eyes.

James and Mary waded through a sea of bottles and reached the door. The sticky deadbolt creaked as James twisted hard with his small hands. Robert lunged from his knees and grabbed Mary's ankle.

"James!" she cried.

The lock snapped open, and James opened the stiff door wide enough to make room for their small frames. Robert lay still behind the door, coughing. James grabbed Mary's hand and tried to drag her away from Robert who chuckled on the floor with his face pressed against the carpet.

"Ow! He won't let go!"

James guided her hands to the window frame beside the door. "Hold this!" James barked before he squeezed himself through the opening and disappeared.

"James! Wait!" she pleaded with tears.

He flew over the patio and into the woods before skidding to a halt and sprinting back toward the house. James slammed his body shoulder-first into the door, and it swung hard into the living room, stopping with a vibrating thud as it slammed into Robert's head. The hand around Mary's ankle fell limp. James wrapped his arms around her, pulled her around himself, and shoved her out the door.

"Run!" he called after her as the bottles behind him surged into a wave.

Suddenly Robert's hand was around James' wrist with crushing power. Robert tried to pull him into the house, but James latched onto the door frame and pulled against him. Robert stepped from behind the door with blood trickling over his brow and his hatred pounding in the vein on his forehead.

James ignored the intense pain radiating from his wrist, his arm like a twig ready to snap. He looked into the eyes of the man whose voice had haunted him in the dark. Time stood still.

James shed a single tear and softened his voice. "I'm sorry this happened to you."

Robert's eyes widened.

"I'm sorry this is who you became."

Robert unclenched his teeth.

James' left arm trembled as he held onto the door frame with little strength left, his right shoulder aching for relief. "I know it was hard losing Mom. And I want you to know… that I love you."

Robert's empty eyes clouded. His jaw shook. He shut his eyes tightly and pushed out a stream of tears. He moaned and released James' wrist. As Robert fell backward sobbing, James tumbled backward over the porch and left his feet. James watched in midair as the house bent and twisted and crumpled like a crushed piece of paper. In only a second, it collapsed into itself like a dying star, and James hit the ground flat on his back.

He stared straight into the sky and caught his breath. The tops of tall pines swayed in his peripheral vision. A playful breeze cooled his face. Fear slowly lifted from his heart.

Thank You.

Mary's erratic breathing caught James' attention. He rolled onto his elbow to look in the direction of her gasps. Mary sat with her arms around her knees, rocking feverishly while she glared through James. She mumbled to herself, raising her voice just enough for him to hear the words "disappeared" and "crazy."

"Mary…" He started at his deepened voice. He pushed himself to his feet and wobbled when he stretched to his full height, looking down at the frightened girl. "Mary."

She stilled herself and looked up. "What just happened? Where did the house go? What happened to you? W-Was that real? Is that real?"

James turned to follow her outstretched index finger. A wide headstone rested a few yards away under the drooping branches of a pine tree. He immediately recognized the shape and design of the shiny granite marker. His parents' names stood on either side of his family name in bold black letters.

He looked back at Mary who waited eagerly for an answer. He smiled before walking to her side and sitting beside her on a patch of grass. James looked down at her with compassion swelling in his heart. "Are you okay, Mary?"

Her eyes filled with another wave of tears. "I think so." She hugged her knees closer. "You were a kid. And then your mom was sick, and your dad… You forgot who I was."

"I forgot." He put his arm around her. "I got lost there for a little while." He waited for her eyes to meet his. "I'm sorry."

"Are *you* okay?" she asked.

"I am." He blew out a deep breath. "Most of what just happened really *did* happen… a long time ago. It just happened a lot slower. It was the worst time of my life." He turned his head toward the empty space where the house stood only a moment before. "I never would have wanted to come back here... to this time... to this place. I'm sorry you had to experience that."

"I'm sorry you had to live through it. There was so much pain in that house."

"There was. It was hard." He looked over at the gravestone. "My mom really suffered... and my dad broke. He was hard enough to live with before. My mom was so loving, so kind. She was everything to me. And I stayed out of my dad's way. When she died... Dad was there... and I wished he wasn't." Sadness swept over his countenance, and he shook his head. "I swore I would never be like him. I wasn't. I'm *not*." He stood up, still studying the gravesite. "But I thought that if I wasn't cruel to my own family... I thought that would be enough. I didn't yell. I wasn't a drunk. I was mostly easygoing... but I still checked out." He turned to Mary and offered her his hand. She stood up, calm and collected. "What I realize now is that I didn't just need my father to stop being who he was... I needed him to *start* being my dad." He dropped his head. "A man isn't defined by what he *isn't*... but what he *is*."

They walked to the graves and stood side by side. James stared for a while at the words "loving husband and father."

"One of these people filled my life with joy... and the other tried to drain it all out." He looked into Mary's eyes. "My daughter deserves better than I had. She deserves better than who I've been." He smiled with a weary sadness. "It's time for me to make things right."

As she lifted her own smile, it filled with new energy. "Let's go find her."

They looked down together, and the gravesite was gone.

* * *

Back on the path, the golden rays that danced through the pine branches had turned pearly white. James' close inspection revealed the living air swirling around each pine needle. The long road eased from side to side as before, boasting no unusual features. Several times, James brushed off the thought that the road may never end, like a bottomless pit.

"Should we agree to keep our eyes on the path?" Mary smiled and playfully pushed James.

"Maybe you're right." James sighed.

"Hey, sarge." She patted his arm. "It's okay. We're gonna be fine. I've got your back."

He found a smile of his own. "I'm really glad you do. If I didn't have you back at that house… I might have never left. Who knows how long I could have been stuck in that nightmare?"

"I won't lie and tell you I enjoyed it. I'm having a hard time pushing it out of my mind… but I'm glad I was there for your sake."

James squeezed her shoulder. "Me, too."

"If we were *really* thinking though…" She grinned wide.

"What?"

"We would've grabbed that pie on the way out."

James laughed deeply. "No, no, no… The pie *definitely* would've disappeared."

Mary's giggles echoed through the woods.

"I may never eat apple pie again," he said.

"Ice cream though…" Her giggles continued.

"Ice cream stays."

"Ice cream is forever, James."

James pondered the pattern of events since his arrival in the clearing. One bizarre event after another had kept him reeling. But each moment had marked him, and he knew that he would never be the same again. The little girl beside him brought with her joy that could only be from God. But the Mary that had faded into the darkness, whisked away by an otherworldly evil, kept his feet moving forward—and kept his heart unsettled. What else would it take to find her?

He felt his knees weaken at the thought of another nightmare ahead.

God, I don't know what's next, but I need Your strength.

He glanced down at his pocket for validation. The path narrowed gradually, but its light remained bright and cheery. The woods held an air of mystery but no gloom. Flowers began to pepper the forest floor, starting with gradients of white and yellow. When dull blues and purples arrived, dark hardwoods were as prevalent as the familiar pines. The canopy over the path leaned farther down the deeper they traveled, as if the forest grew tired. The idea slipped into James' mind that they were not in fact passing through a forest but entering one. He wondered now not what was on the other side of the woods but what was at the heart of them.

"Are there no animals here?" Mary spun as she walked, looking overhead for signs of life.

"Hmm, it's pretty quiet."

James curled his nose. The air grew stale as the trees in front of them drew closer. The way forward was unclear. Mary's head swiveled from side to side. The path's surroundings changed quickly enough to slow their pace. The road seemed to divide two emerging forests that stood guard against each other. On the left pleasant, twisting oaks and on the right indiscernible ashen trees, gnarled and withered. With wary, roving eyes, James and Mary arrived at a fork, with a path left leading into hopeful golden light and a path right with a distant blue haze and an unspoken unfriendliness.

Mary veered to the left side of the main road as the path began to divide, and James watched the smoking flames from his pocket drift right. He stopped and spoke up before she could commit to the golden light.

"Hold on, Mary."

"What's up?"

"I think it's time I showed you something."

She spun on her toes and flitted to his side.

He put his arm around her shoulder. "Walk with me."

James strolled with her to the center of the fork and drew the map from his pocket. He unfolded it carefully and held it low enough for Mary to see. James stood silent and watched blue wisps of smoke dance over the map's surface while orange fire traced every curling vapor. The strokes of ink pulsed with a supernatural glow.

"So, you're telling me… you've had a map this whole time?" She leaned close. "A detailed map. And you didn't think I should know that. And you didn't think we should be consulting it." Her voice grew louder. "*Why* did you wait until now to show me this?" She held up her hands as if holding the magnitude of his omission over her head like a boulder, her eyes wide, her mouth agape.

"I'm sorry. I… wasn't sure how to explain."

"How to explain," she repeated. "How to explain that you have a map. Please tell me how that makes sense." Her head cocked and her eyes rolled high.

"Well, Mary, it's not a… it's not your average map."

"No, the average map is on your phone, and it has a little British voice that tells you where to go. *This* map is actually relevant to this very strange place." Her pace quickened. "James! Don't you think it would've put my mind at ease to know that you could see what was beyond that island? Don't you think I could've used a little more hope?"

"I'm sorry, Mary! I guess I didn't think of that. I… Maybe I was afraid of what you would think."

"You're making no *sense!* Please. Please make sense. Why are you being weird about this?" Mary palmed her temples and pulled her hairline back.

"You don't see it do you?" James looked for a glimpse of understanding in her expression.

"See *what*, James?" She looked at him with total exasperation.

"Look down, Mary—closely."

She scanned the map, shaking her head. "Help me out, James."

"I can see…"

"I see it!" she squeaked.

"You do?" James' jolted with excitement.

"Here we are!"

"Here we—huh?" James' face contorted.

"Look!" She skimmed the map with her index finger. "The island… the beach where we landed. Look, the rocks! The *pier*, James! We went this way…" She traced the last several miles.

"And here we are!" She landed on the fork in the path where they stood.

"Here we are." James' jaw hung loose. "Go figure."

She laid her hand on his arm. "Why didn't you show me this? Why didn't we use it?"

James paused and prepared himself to sound ridiculous. "I *have* been using it."

"Huh? You've been sneaking it out?"

"No, I... I don't have to look at it to follow it. I know that sounds *crazy*. But this map is a lot more than it seems. There's a power, an energy that comes from it. I can literally see it right now."

Mary looked at James as she had when he was a little boy trying to save his mother. "James... I don't understand. This is just a map."

"Mary, there's a... force that comes from this map. It literally looks like smoke and fire. It shows which way to go. It makes new paths. *New* paths, Mary, where the trees have to move out of the way! It *made* the boat that took me to you. It saved our raft. It even destroyed the voices!"

Mary grimaced more sharply with every word. "James, am I losing you? Are we back in that house again? You don't sound like yourself."

"Mary, no... I have to be honest with you. I know how it sounds. If you'll let me, I'll show you... Mary, this map came from God."

"God..." Mary's countenance wilted. "I feel like I'm arguing with my mom again."

"It's true, Mary. Haven't I earned your trust?"

She sighed and studied the map. "Okay, James." She smiled

up at him. "It's fine. Maybe you know something I don't know. That's fine. Let's just… keep walking, and maybe you can show me what you mean." She took several steps backward toward the path on the left.

"Mary, wait." James glanced at the glowing flames that soared toward the path on the right. "We can't go that way."

"No, James." She returned to his side and traced the pathways on the map. "See? The path that goes left leads out of the woods. There's open country with hills and rivers. The rest of the map is this way. The path that goes right leads into these dark woods and *nowhere else*. Look, there are steep cliffs all around this forest and no other way out." She looked up with begging eyes. "The only reason you would go right is if you want to stay in those woods." She gazed down the dark, narrow path with ashen trees. "That's not somewhere I want to stay."

"What if my daughter is in there?" He hoped that the concern in his voice would disarm her.

She touched his cheek. "That's why we're here. And *you're* the reason *I'm* here. But I'm struggling with this. You said you want to follow this map. The map leads left. I'm going left, James. If it doesn't work out, I'll walk right back here with you, and we'll go down that creepy path together. I owe you that. But I have to see what's this way first."

She was jogging down the left path before James could think. He furiously folded the map and stuffed it into his pocket as he walked after her. She disappeared around the left path's first bend.

"Mary, hold on!"

He leaned into a jog. No response. He gained speed and trotted around the bend and into a small clearing with a tamped floor of mingled dirt and grass. Several openings split from this clearing and ran through the woods.

He stopped at the center and glared down each path. "Mary?" The hair on his arms and neck raised. "Mary!" His voice echoed through the trees.

He stood still and allowed his hearing to search for footsteps. Instead, a chilling breeze carried the sound of Mary's voice to his ears.

"Mary!"

"Hey, Daddy." Her voice was faint; it wasn't lifted with the intent of reaching him over a distance. "What are you doing?" Her voice came from his left.

He turned and walked toward the space between two tall pines. There stood Mary down a new path, facing away from him, but her clothes were different. Beside her was a red recliner, rocking gently.

His heart thumped in his ear. He walked between the trees, and his vision blurred and waved, like he had plunged his head underwater. The sensation lasted only a second, and his curiosity pulled him down the path and into a new grassy clearing where Mary was waiting.

She wasn't alone.

TWELVE

That's my chair. As soon as the thought had entered his mind, his own voice filled his ears and crawled over his skin.

"Oh, hi, baby girl. Sorry I didn't hear you."

"It's okay, Daddy. What are you doing?"

An arm from the chair reached out and patted her back. "Baby, I'm just watching the news."

"Okay."

James pushed his trembling body into motion and crept along the outer edge of the clearing until he could see their faces. There sat his own likeness in his red leather chair, Mary staring forward beside him. The color of the glow on their faces changed abruptly every few seconds as the camera shots on a television changed. James glanced in front of them at a small TV that was plugged into nothing but displaying his old favorite cable news show. The anchor droned on. Afraid to move again, James stared back at a younger, thinner version of himself.

After a minute of silence, he had gathered the courage to interrupt the scene. "Mary," he whispered.

"Dad…"

"Mary!" James called out.

Oblivious to James' call, she looked at his younger self and waited for a response.

"Oh, hey, Mary." He answered reluctantly, his eyes transfixed on the news.

"Dad, would you play a game with me?"

"Sweet girl, I'm so tired. I had a really hard day today, and my back is hurting. You know how that is. Let's do it another time."

James placed a palm on his back and thought of the injury that had made back pain a regular part of his life since college.

"Okay, Dad." She started toward the opening where James had entered but stopped short and turned back to face her father. "I'll pray for you."

Her words were loud enough to be heard, but they fell on closed ears. Mary stood staring at the back of the chair, her expression more downcast by the second.

James walked closer to his former self unnoticed and stood between him and the TV. The man in the chair gazed through James with a look of utter contentment while the little girl behind him stood wanting.

"Mary!" sang a sweet voice from behind her.

Gloria.

Mary's face lifted a feeble smile at the sound of her mother's call. "Coming!" She skipped through the opening and out of sight.

James stepped close and looked down at himself. "Blind fool." He blinked away a pool of tears. "She just wants to be heard… She just wants to be loved. She needs you!" He thought of attempting to strike himself on the jaw but took a deep breath instead. "You look so peaceful, James. And what has it cost you? What has it cost her?"

He trudged back through the opening, up the path, and into the first clearing. His vision waved, and he started again. No Mary in sight.

Familiar laughter rode a light breeze into the clearing from the opposite direction.

"Where am I?" He directed the question to his pocket, but no guidance came. "God, I don't want to do this." James' feet ignored his statement and carried him toward another opening. Again, his vision distorted as he passed between towering pines onto a pathway which led to another clearing.

At the center was a full-size bed with four tall, ornate posts and all-white bedding. Gloria and Mary lay on their backs side by side, talking and laughing like the best of friends, only this Mary was a teenager. A long, wavy ponytail hung over the side of the bed and almost touched the grass.

"Stop!" Mary giggled with an awkward voice. "It's not like I'm gonna marry him!"

"Oh, I don't know," Gloria teased. "You marry the pastor's son, and I'll get all the choir solos I want."

"Mom!"

"Mrs. Mary Lamb."

"Ew, Mom. Let it go, please."

"You'll *know* that he's the one, if you're willing to suffer through the jokes." She belly-laughed, and Mary joined her.

James tiptoed close enough to see the joy in their eyes. Gloria's crystal blue eyes had led the effort of winning his heart years ago. She looked as beautiful as ever.

Mary looked at her mother. "I love you."

"I love you too, honey… even if you don't marry that boy and have a flock of little Lambs."

The laughter turned into a tickle fight, and James couldn't help but laugh himself, though he felt like he was miles away from them.

How did I miss this?

He thought of the closeness he had already developed with little Mary. In just a few days, he was closer to her than to the Mary he'd known for nineteen years. Guilt seized his soul again.

A door appeared beyond the bed and opened just as quickly as it materialized. Gloria and Mary sat up straight to face another James from another time.

"Mary." His tone held frustration but restraint.

Mary acknowledged him with her undivided attention and waited for him to continue.

"Can you tell me why I just found the car unlocked *again?*"

Mary answered timidly. "I'm sorry, Dad."

He squinted and drew in his lips. "You know, that's what you said the last two times I found the car unlocked. Do I need to tell you again about what can happen if the car is left unlocked? Or *maybe* I need to make sure you don't see the keys for a month."

Mary looked down. "I'm sorry."

Gloria weaved her head in an apparent attempt to gain James' attention, but he ignored her.

He stared at Mary's face until she looked up. "I didn't cause the problem, so I'm not solving it. It's unlocked right now."

Mary hesitated.

"Go," he huffed.

She glided past him while he held onto the doorknob.

Gloria spoke as he started to shut the door. "James."

He raised his brows to invite her to speak.

"Why so rough?" The question sounded like an olive branch.

"If I'm not tough, she won't grow up."

"You've got to show her love, not just tough."

He shut the door just slowly enough for his retort to enter the room. "She knows I love her."

Gloria looked straight up and sighed. "God, help him. I don't know how."

James stood behind her and watched her wipe the tears from her cheeks. She lowered her head and whispered, "Help me, too."

Why do I feel like my father was just here? James hung his head.

The sound of shattering dishes stole his attention and whipped his head over his shoulder. He shook the desire to comfort Gloria out of his head and jogged back down the path and into the clearing, his head swimming through the invisible gateway again.

At the center stood the family kitchen with ivory cabinets and an island. Gloria leaned against a granite countertop, fighting for breath, wearing her favorite lavender headscarf. Shards of broken plates covered the matted dirt and grass.

Mary rushed into the room from thin air. "Mom! Are you okay?"

Gloria nodded rapidly. "Yeah, yeah, I'm okay."

"What are you doing? I can help you!"

"I know, baby."

"That's why I took some days off, Mom." She reached under her mother's shoulder and steered her toward another opening.

"I told you not to do that. It's not easy to catch up in college, honey."

"I talked it out with all my professors *and* my advisor. Stop worrying."

Gloria looked at her. "I'll stop worrying right now when you promise me that you won't take any more days off, no matter what."

"Okay, Mom, fine! No more days off. When is Dad coming home? He's not working today, right?"

James padded a few yards behind them, avoiding the broken plates. He winced through another cloaked doorway between two pines. Mary helped Gloria into the disheveled master bed after moving aside a tray table.

"He'll be home soon, I'm sure, Mary."

"Where did he go?"

"I don't think he said." Gloria settled under her mother's patchwork quilt.

"Mom... he should be here when he can."

Gloria brushed Mary's cheek. "Baby, this is hard for him."

"Hard for *him?*"

Gloria grimaced and held up a palm. "I know, Mary. But there's a lot you don't know. Your dad has been through a lot, not the least of which is losing his mom to colon cancer. He's been here before."

Mary set her jaw and leaned close to her. "He doesn't get to hide."

Gloria smiled and held Mary's hands. "We're all just doing the best we can."

"*You* deserve *his* best."

She pulled Mary down into a warm embrace. "I have the world, baby girl."

James wanted to turn and see himself walk into the room with all the love Gloria could ever want, but he knew that no one else was coming. The yellow glow of the forest illuminated Gloria's tear-soaked cheeks. His knees wobbled under the weight of his selfish choices.

"I'm sorry," he said aloud where no one but God could hear him.

I was there. I was a husband. I was a father. I was neither.

"What was I thinking?"

"Oh, James… James…" lilted a song on the breeze.

Mary.

He barged back into the first clearing and called out. "Mary?"

"Jimmity-Jame-James…"

He chortled and shuffled to the center of the clearing, scanning from path to path to see her arrival. He dried his face with his sleeves.

"I found someone…" she sang.

A wave of concern washed his relief aside. "You found a person?"

"No, James, I found a magic dragon." The song was over, and the sarcasm was back. "I *found* a friend." Mary emerged from a central opening, and a few steps behind her strolled a man with dark hair and piercing green eyes.

James froze. "Zell," he whispered, his eyes wide. A chill traveled his height. His hair stood on end.

Zell strode forward and stopped in front of him with a gleeful grin stretched across his thin face. "Hello, there, friend. My name is Zell."

James clenched his fingers and his teeth. "Are you kidding me?"

"Oh, no, friend. It's an unusual name, but it certainly belongs to me."

"Zell, this is my friend James."

Mary's voice failed to capture a sliver of James' attention. His eyes bored deep into Zell's, his body tensed and ready for a fight.

Zell maintained a smug expression. "This most delightful young lady found me wandering in these woods, totally lost. I trust you've found this place to be quite disorienting as well."

"James?" Mary leaned in front of him with furrowed brows. "You don't look so good."

James looked down at her and found no words to send to his tongue.

"Friend, I hope I haven't imposed on your peace."

Mary touched Zell's arm while glaring at James. "No, we're glad to have you. James, is something wrong? What's with the scowl?"

What do I do?

He glanced down at his pocket and then up at Zell who had followed his eyes. His devious smile made clear that the river James had plunged into wasn't water under this bridge.

James forced himself to breathe slowly. "I'm okay, Mary."

"A lovely name, Mary." Zell's smile crawled even wider.

"Then why are you acting so weird? Did something happen?" Mary pressed.

"Actually, yes, something strange happened." He reached a hand in her direction without moving his eyes. "Why don't you stand behind me, and I'll explain."

Zell's eyes danced at James' request.

"Um, what's going on? Wait, who's that?" Mary gawked

behind James.

"What's she doing here?" The familiar voice sent a tremor over James' body. The subtle sound of hissing, cracking, and moaning followed. He peeled his eyes away from Zell and turned. A slender woman with amber eyes stood in the opening before him with black, thorny vines, as thick as cobras, twisting and writhing around her entire body.

THIRTEEN

"You're alive." James bolted toward Mary and slammed into a barrier between the trees. What was an open portal was now a cold sheet of invisible glass. He stumbled backward with a groan, holding his forehead after the jarring collision, and fell into the man behind him. Zell caught James with a wide stance and wrapped his arms around him to break his fall.

Before standing him upright, he whispered in his ear with a playful rasp. "Careful there, friend."

James snatched himself into a guarded position facing him with a glower.

"You shouldn't be here." Mary's voice spun him around again. Her cold, vacant look offered no hope for reconciliation. She looked past him. "And neither should she."

Little Mary cleared her throat. "Excuse me, miss. Is there some problem that you have with me? You're welcome to direct your concerns right here."

Mary ignored her and directed an icy glare at her father. "You can't help her. Did you really think you could make everything better like *this?*"

"I'm just trying to be a better man." His voice cracked. His heart pounded. "I know I don't deserve the chance to make things right with you. But you deserve a better father. I'm trying to become that person… because I love you."

"Well, I hate you." Her calm reply was contrasted by a thunderous lash from one of the dark vines, a strike that landed on the invisible barrier between them. The impact sent splinters over the surface with a sound like cracking ice.

James and little Mary flinched. Zell suppressed a low chuckle.

James' heart ached with his head, but he held his composure. "You have a lot of reasons to resent me, reasons that I've been giving you since you were a little girl."

"Stop." She held her arms out with her palms up. Vines spiraled around her arms, thorns grazing and barely breaking her skin, leaving red, razor-thin tracks. "You don't get to make speeches. You don't get to tell me what I deserve or what I need. You don't know who I am."

"I want to know."

"You don't get to know." Another lash sent more cracks across the barrier.

"You're not yourself. Let me come to you," he begged.

"I needed you then." She nodded at little Mary. "But that time is gone, and now I don't."

Another lash. James could barely see her through the mangled web of broken glass.

He offered a final quiet plea. "Don't lose yourself in what you've lost. I did."

After a moment of silence, Mary whimpered from the other side. "All I want to lose is you. Just leave me alone."

With the last three softly spoken words, three devastating

whips from the thorny vines finished off the barrier. The window fell into shattered pieces and vanished before they could touch the ground. Mary was gone.

James' weak knees threatened to buckle, but he held himself upright through waves of despair. Painful throbs on his forehead dizzied him, and he fought to catch his breath.

"Well, that was entertaining." Zell's tone was cordial.

James spun around awkwardly, his urgency greater than his energy.

Zell stood with little Mary under his left arm, his hand clasped over her mouth, her feet off the ground. Mary's amber eyes watered. Zell's green eyes burned with hostility.

He looked down at James' pocket and grinned. James' eyes widened, and he grasped the fabric over his pocket, knowing that he would find nothing. Zell reveled in the moment, threw back his black hair, and laughed obnoxiously. He lifted the map with his right hand like a trophy.

"You've got to pay attention, James."

James held out his empty hand. "Just don't hurt her." His words squeaked out.

"Oh, James, you invaded my beautiful sanctuary. You destroyed my home!" He looked down at trembling Mary. "He blew it up!"

Zell slid the map into his pocket and stood up straight. He evened his expression and his tone of voice at James. "So now I'm going to take what you love. You took *my peace*, after all."

Zell backpedaled to the opening behind him.

"No!" James lunged into a sprint in pursuit.

Zell disappeared through the opening's invisible doorway just before James barged through. He stumbled forward. His vision adjusted. Another rounded clearing, and Mary and Zell weren't in it. The ground rumbled. Branches snapped behind James. Dirt pelted his back and neck. He turned. Whole trees had shot up from the ground and blocked the opening he had just used.

"Oh, no."

The woods around him squirmed, and the earth shook. Zell cackled. James loped around the perimeter as trunks and branches raced to seal every opening large enough for his escape. Again, he found himself trapped in a prison, this time by a host of trees under Zell's control. His enemy squealed with delight.

"Look familiar, James?" Zell gloated out of sight, his voice echoing all around the clearing. "Only now you don't have a magic map. Now you're out of luck. No way out."

"Don't hurt Mary!" he pled.

"Oh, this little thing? Hmm… I like her spirit. But she'll just slow me down. I've got work to do."

Mary yelped and then screamed.

"No!" James' protest was futile.

After a rustle in the trees overhead, a long, knotty oak bough appeared through the canopy with little Mary trapped in a tangle of its branches. It hovered above the center of the clearing.

"I know where she is, James. And I'm going to her. I'll send my regards."

Terror filled James' heart. "Don't you—"

"This one can suffer with you."

The branches overhead released little Mary, and she fell shrieking toward the forest floor. James dove onto his back beneath her in time to break her fall. She tumbled over his body and rolled into a crumpled heap. Zell's laughter trailed away on the breeze.

James crawled over Mary. "Are you okay? Please be okay." He gathered her in his arms.

She groaned faintly. "I think I'm okay." She flexed her back and winced with her eyes still closed.

"I'm so sorry, Mary." James heaved to stifle the sob in his chest. "I don't know how to get out of this. Without the map, there's nothing I can do."

She smiled and looked up and him. "You mean this?" She pulled the map from her pocket.

"Mary! No way!" James hugged her tightly.

"Hey, okay! Take it easy. That's what you hired me for." She straightened her back and looked at the folded map. "It's still just a…"

Mary stared stunned as blue smoke and orange flame swirled around the map, dancing gracefully in front of her eyes.

"You see it? You see it!" James beamed with excitement.

"Uh…" Mary had no witty remark.

The map's energy gathered in a sphere of silent strength and rushed toward the ground in front of them. Earth and stone unfurled before their eyes. The ground vibrated beneath them as the map carved a wide tunnel through the darkness below. Rocks split, roots snapped, and dirt sifted downward. A way of escape.

A distant screech from Zell sent James and Mary scrambling from their knees to their feet and into the new descending pathway. The trees creaked and crunched into action, leaning and bowing to reach after the prisoners. As James and Mary found a running stride, roots burst through the tunnel walls, and branches plunged through the skylight at their master's command. The path continued to unfold at a steep decline ahead of them.

Mary screamed after every drawn breath, uncarved earth and rock always feet in front of her, smoke and fire flying forward. James gasped and grunted ahead of the ever-lengthening roots and branches bent on their capture.

Just like last time.

"Mary, you're gonna have to stop," he blurted.

"Are you crazy?" she barked, barreling deeper.

"Trust me, Mary! Stop, turn, and hold the map in front of you!"

"You've done this before?"

"Yes! I know! No more secrets!"

"Holy Christmas, here we go." She locked her jaw and performed a leaping turn toward the violent pursuit. With her eyes shut tight she held the map straight out and landed on her feet. James darted around her and braced her upright.

Out of the map a blinding and deafening inferno roared up the tunnel in an instant. Every branch and root disintegrated into ash, all the way to the light of the clearing. The ground below shuddered, and the ground above crumbled. Zell's piercing scream was cut off. The light above gave way to darkness as the tunnel behind their escape collapsed.

The orange blaze vanished. The blue smoke faded. The grumbling earth settled still. James and Mary gasped for air in utter darkness.

"James?" Mary's voice shook with urgency.

"Well done, Mary. Don't worry." He patted her back. "He's gotten us this far."

The sound of rustling parchment rose above their heavy breathing. The map flickered faintly and cast a low light on

Mary's face. It slowly unfolded itself in her open hand and lifted into the air, shining brighter as it spun and shifted without contact. It curled into a cylindrical shape and stretched a single strip of parchment over the top. Faster and faster it rotated while a small orb of radiant fire grew into a flame the size of a fist, hovering untouched in the center of the newly formed lantern. A brilliant glow illuminated the walls of the small cave around James and Mary, the lines of ink casting a mesmerizing show of spinning shadows.

The map floated slowly toward the ground, and Mary grasped the parchment handle that had formed over the lantern. Peering over the map's edges, she studied the levitating fire with her mouth agape. She moved the map left and right and failed to upset the flame's decided place. Mary stood silent and shook her head with her eyes fixed on the source of supernatural light.

"I've never seen anything like this." Her voice was calm and sure now. "This isn't just… paranormal." She passed her palm beneath the lantern, testing its warmth. "This is divine."

Pure satisfaction filled James' heart. "Yes, it is."

"I understand why you didn't try to explain this… until I pushed you. How do you explain this?"

He chuckled and shrugged. "I can't tell you how relieved I am that you can see it. This map has led me through impossible circumstances. It led me to God. And then it led me to you."

A shadow of sadness passed over Mary's face. "I won't lie to you. When you talk about God, something inside me bristles. It's uncomfortable." She looked back at the lantern. "But I can't deny what my eyes are telling me. Something is happening right here that defies explanation. I don't have a reason in my mind that what's happening in my hand *isn't* God."

James squeezed her shoulder.

"But for now…" She handed him the lantern. "I need to work with what I can see."

"Okay, Mary." He sighed and glanced around the caved-in tunnel. "Ready to get going?"

"Lead on, Your Royal Highness."

James turned away from Mary and flourished the lantern in front of himself. Instantly a much larger tunnel loudly burrowed straight ahead with high, flat walls and a smooth, stone floor.

FOURTEEN

James paused and filled his lungs with musty air while he massaged his tender forehead. He held the lantern out in front of himself, hoping to see farther down the underground pathway before proceeding. The view ahead was less than inviting. Had the path not been carved out by the map, he might have stayed rooted to the ground beneath him.

His lip curled without his permission. "Something is… old about this place."

"Didn't it just appear?" Mary lingered behind him.

"Or maybe it was just revealed." He bobbed the lantern. "This map is always up to something." He sighed and shrugged. "God knows what else we can take, I guess. Let's go."

Off they walked over the stone floor. Each step reverberated off the hard surfaces that surrounded them. The lantern swung before James and swept the walls with a steady rhythm of surging light.

"James, look." Mary pointed to the walls. First one line, then two, then many. Intricate engraved designs ran over the walls in every direction, all composed of thin lines, precisely carved into the earthen passage. As they walked the path, studying the carvings, they missed the floor's transition to an ornate stone tile pattern until its texture under their shoes drew their eyes. The farther they traveled, the more effort of composition was evident. Even the ceiling was smooth and without blemish, though unspoiled by artistry. James decided that hands were responsible for this craftsmanship. Perhaps the map had led them to the end of a work in progress that had begun from the other direction.

Dim, gold lights appeared in the distance along the walls and mingled with the map's broad glow. James and Mary continued in silence, save their echoing steps, until a breeze carried a faint foul odor to them.

James raised his brows at Mary. "You know… if we weren't led here by the map… I'd be freaking out right about now."

Mary laughed nervously. "I hope this thing doesn't hesitate to protect us from the monsters we're probably walking toward." She frowned. "Didn't you say it *made* the boat that brought you to me?"

"That's right."

"And then it left you boatless, lying on your back on the beach?"

"Uh, yeah."

Mary shrugged. "So, it's got jokes."

James let out a breath slowly. "It's got jokes."

The lights ahead proved to be oil lamps shaped from clay and set into the stone walls. As they passed the first lamp, Mary pointed to the carvings on the wall, which had begun to lose their skillful precision. The lines waved and varied in depth, some threatening to collide with each other.

The lantern's fiery sphere dimmed. James peeked over the

edge of the parchment and watched their light shrink. *Oh, come on...* With a puff of scattering blue smoke, it disappeared, and the map noisily twisted and flapped itself into its familiar folded shape in James' hand without a hint of warmth.

"Jokes," said Mary impassively.

"Jokes," James repeated.

Their eyes fought to adjust to the lower light provided by the clay lamps which had been placed with conservative distance from each other, leaving stretches of total darkness for them to walk through. Where the floor could not be seen, James stayed ahead of Mary and groped with his toes out in front of him, in case some pitfall lay in their path. Surrounding each lamp was a patch of carvings, each cruder than the last. Skillful design gradually gave way to haphazard scrawling.

"How about some English?" Mary had stopped to inspect a single word scraped into the stone wall under a lamp.

Peace.

"Do you hear something?"

James waited for the echo from Mary's question to die. A far-off muted mumbling took its place. They stared into each other's eyes with their ears aimed down the corridor. James' mind raced to process the sound, hoping for a natural explanation. The more they listened, the clearer the voice became and the more the sound struck a tone of distress.

"Is someone in trouble?" James waited for Mary's interpretation.

"Are *we* in trouble?"

Good question.

"Just go with it," James said coldly as he broke into an even stride down the path through the dim light and into the darkness, the sound of his steps bouncing off the walls after the mysterious voice.

Mary scampered behind him with quiet mumbling of her own. "Are we sure? Are we totally sure that we should just walk right into this? Is there something wrong with a more calculated approach... like, maybe, quieter ste—" She rammed into James' back.

He stood still in the darkness between lamps and listened. The voice had been replaced by approaching footsteps. Mary whined, and James reached back to rest a hand on her arm.

The voice returned, louder and more confident. Only a few intelligible words broke through the echoes. "Quiet... alone... never..." Then a figure strode into the dull light four lamps away. He leaned far forward with disheveled hair and a scraggly beard, all gray.

As he stepped into the next patch of darkness, he raised his voice to a jarring roar. "...doesn't *belong* in my *home!*"

Mary squeaked, and a crippling chill seized James. They gripped each other tightly in the gloom. When the stranger's scowl burst into the light of the next lamp, Mary grabbed the back of James' shirt and tugged violently.

James dropped his head in her direction and whispered, "Against the wall."

He slid to the left, and Mary scrambled to the right. The man stomped through the darkness, growling his frustration. James focused on regulating his breath. Mary whimpered on the other side of the path. James released the quietest shush he could.

Into the light the man barked again. "This is unacceptable!"

James clung to the wall. *Please, God, help us.*

"Who thinks they can come into my home..."

The steps thundered into the darkness.

"I'm not going anywhere, and if anyone thinks they have the right to invade my privacy…"

James squinted as the man's wrinkled face entered the last light. His jaw was locked. His eyes were focused forward. His angry words were spent for the moment.

Mary, hold your breath.

James stilled himself completely. His heart pounded in his ears. The man plodded past them without hesitation. He broke into the next light as Mary released her breath loudly enough for James to hear. The man slid to a stop under the lamp's haunting glow.

Oh, no.

He turned slowly and stared down the tunnel he had just traveled with his eyes barely open. His brows and nose cast unkind shadows over his face. He stood still and waited. James stared into the black where Mary hid. The man breathed deeply and muttered something too low to understand. Then he spun on his heels and marched on, farther up the great hall, away from James and Mary.

They waited still and silent until he was almost out of sight.

"Are you okay?" James whispered.

"Are you *kidding* me?" she whispered back.

James doubled over and sighed his relief. "Let's go."

They rejoined in the center of the path and hurried down the corridor with the softest steps they could manage, now sure that the path was clear of obstacles.

"He's gonna find a collapsed tunnel. We've gotta be faster than him," James hissed.

"I knew I should've brought my spear."

"It never would've survived that storm."

"I'm making one as soon as we get out of here."

More words peppered the walls around the lamps. Mary whispered as many as she could as they went.

"Comfort... Serenity... Sanctum... What a piece of work, this guy."

"I'm more than happy to leave him to his iss—" James tripped over his feet in the dark and hit the stone floor face first. A squawk had escaped his lips before he could restrain it. The scream and the thud took turns reverberating up and down the path walls. James and Mary waited and listened. The echoes tapered and ceased.

"We're good. I'm good." James said weakly. He rubbed his stinging cheek.

They waited in silence until an angry yowl reached them with a rush of wind from where they had come. James stumbled to his feet and into a wall before finding his way forward.

Mary bolted ahead of him. "Come on, move!"

"That's what I'm doing!"

"Do it faster!"

James struggled forward. The screams behind them were joined by resounding footsteps. He glanced over his shoulder in time to see the man's face vanish into a dark void between the lamps. James released a wavering moan.

"James, a room! Hurry up!"

Just ahead, brighter light shone from inside a large room.

"What are you doing here?" wailed the voice behind them.

The room drew close. The man's heavy breathing crept behind James who tried and failed to wriggle his hand into his pocket while he ran.

God...

Mary reached the room and darted right beyond the doorway. James stumbled in, reaching for the map again as he turned. The man let out a low yell and threw himself at James. Mary shrieked as the stranger slammed into James and landed on top of him with all his weight. James' head struck the floor hard enough to blur his vision.

"No! Get off him!"

Mary tried to push the man off James, but he shoved her aside with ease. He raised himself above James and drew back his fist. Blurred vision couldn't hide the fire in the man's eyes.

Then he froze. He let out a fearful groan and pulled himself off James' weak frame. He scooted backward on the floor, shaking his head fiercely.

"No, no, no, no... What is this? *How?*" He sniveled and moaned before turning to Mary and wailing out a loud cry of lament. "*Why...* Who sent you? Oh, God, no..." He wept without restraint.

James lifted himself to a seated position with great effort and grasped the back of his head. When he looked at Mary, who sat on the stone floor a few feet away, she was squinting at the stranger's face.

"Is this..." She looked at James, bewildered. "James, is that *you?*"

James whipped his head toward his attacker and tried to blink away the floaters. His eyes focused. The man's visage brought his father flooding to his mind. He saw Robert's brows and cheeks. He saw Patricia's eyes.

The man stared at the floor through tears. "Why can't I just be free?"

James heard his own voice. "I'd love to tell you that it's not, but I think... this is me."

"Good grief," Mary griped.

James lowered his voice while he rubbed his throbbing head. "The shirt he's wearing is hanging in my closet at home."

The man gazed into another world.

"I don't even like this shirt." James checked his fingers for blood.

The man pinned James with a look of grave sincerity. "You can't be here." He shifted his gaze to Mary and shed another tear. "Mary... Oh, Mary, you shouldn't be here."

Mary tensed and slid backward. "How do you know my name?"

"You're not safe here." He looked back at James and sharpened his tone. "You need to go. Now."

"It's not every day you see yourself without looking in a mirror... James." *This is crazy.* "I'd like to hear a little more than an invitation to leave."

"I don't know, James." Mary now stood a few yards away, staring down at an open sarcophagus made of solid gold, its lid resting askew on top.

James stood slowly and joined Mary to study her discovery. Its shape and design resembled James, expertly crafted with great attention to detail.

Mary grabbed his arm. "I'm not sure we want to be here—especially you."

He glowered at his older counterpart. "What is this?"

Old James stared up at him blankly.

"Hey," he pressed. "What is this place? I think a coffin that has my face on it concerns me."

Old James stood and stepped close to him. He spoke in hushed tones to exclude Mary. "*This* is what I had to do."

An unthinkable idea entered James' mind. "Don't tell me... Do you... *live* in there?" A knot formed in James' stomach.

"Stop looking at me like that." Old James narrowed his eyes. "At least I'm not hurting the people I love."

James' face filled with a mixture of confusion and disgust. "What are you even talking about?"

Old James smirked and folded his arms. "You don't even know what you are, do you?" He wobbled his head. "No, sure you do, James. You just don't want to think about it. I've been there." He poked James' chest with his finger. "You gave up everything for your wife and then for your little girl. You sacrificed it all to make them happy. You've made sure there's peace in your home and harmony in your family. And what do you feel when she chooses God over you every day? What does it take from you when everything revolves around everyone else and you're just an afterthought, a ghost haunting your own home? It hurts, doesn't it?"

James' voice caught.

"Listen to me, James." Old James leaned closer. "You're *angrier* than you realize. You know it. You just don't want to admit it to yourself. You're angry all the time, aren't you? Everything you've lost stays under your skin." He softened his expression and spoke as if to a child. "But you love your family, don't you? They became your world. And you don't want to hurt them." He looked around the tomb and settled his eyes on the coffin. "I don't want to hurt them, James. I love them too much. But I'm so angry. And you know as well as I do... the only way I can control it is to withdraw. I have to protect them."

James looked at him sorrowfully. "But you can't just hide. If you hide, you won't live. And they won't really have you in their lives."

Old James darted his eyes around until a tear formed and fell. "No... No, we're not strong enough."

James grabbed his shirt. "You speak for yourself."

"I am!" Old James bellowed. "If I can't do it, you never will."

"I'm different now."

"Different," he repeated with a short-lived grin. He looked coldly into James' eyes. "You'll always be your father waiting to happen."

James scowled at him. "I think I've heard enough of what you have to say."

"Fine. You can think whatever you want of me." He ripped away from James and moved toward the coffin.

Mary padded behind James and peered around him. James gave her shoulder a reassuring pat.

"But it's love that keeps me here, James," the old man said with his back to them.

"Love?" James smirked. "This isn't love. This is fear. This is shame. This is apathy... coward."

Old James clenched his fists.

James seethed with indignation. "You're just a feckless husband and an absent father."

Old James' shoulders raised. He took several labored breaths before throwing back his head and yelling out. "I told you! She... is *not safe* here!"

He twisted himself around and lunged for Mary, but James caught him with a right hook on the jaw. Old James tumbled onto the floor and sprang up with a growl. He pulled back his fist, but James landed another booming punch, snapping back his head. Old James looked around in a daze. Mary skittered away from the fray.

James stepped back and adjusted his angle carefully. He sprinted at the man he had come to loathe and kicked him forcefully in the chest. Old James toppled backward and landed with a crash inside the sarcophagus, unconscious.

"I'm done with you." James grabbed the golden lid and strained with all his strength. He dragged it over the coffin and sealed the man he used to be inside.

He looked up at Mary who stood wide-eyed with her jaw hanging low.

She shook her head slowly. "Okay. That was awesome. Can we go now?"

FIFTEEN

"Let's get out of here." James scanned the room and spotted an opening behind the coffin. "Does this way look pleasant enough?"

"Who cares? Let's go."

Mary followed him through a narrow doorway with a low arch. James ducked to creep down the cramped tunnel crudely carved through the rock. No lamps lit this corridor, so James pulled the map from his pocket as the light behind them faded. Instantly it resumed the form of a lantern with a round, flickering flame at its heart. They moved at an eager pace. The thought of his worst nature rousing pressed James onward. The foul smell weakened and fell from their minds.

"Hey, you." Mary tapped James' back. "You're acting okay, but nobody would be okay after what just happened."

James wiped his brow. "I'm fine."

"I don't think you are."

"Well, I am."

"Not convinced." She wrapped her fingers around his arm. "You don't have to let his lies get to you. Clearly that wasn't who you really are."

James rubbed his throbbing head and looked back at her. "That was me. That was me in every way, Mary." He faced the way forward again. "I spent my childhood hiding from my father. And when I thought I was free, I got my own family… and then I started hiding from them. The truth is… I've always been just as angry as my dad." He strode faster.

"You're nothing like that monster." She skipped to keep up.

"That's just it. I wanted more than anything to be nothing like him, but the same tortured, self-loathing was right there, boiling under the surface. I didn't lash out like he did, but I didn't deal with it either. I just hid away."

Mary grabbed his arm and dragged him to a halt.

He turned to face her. His unreleased tears glinted in the firelight. "That tomb felt very familiar to me."

"Well, you're not hiding now."

"I'm trying not to." He smiled before looking off. "It's hard to face facts, but they're staring me in the face. That man, that James back there… He was wrong about hiding, but he wasn't wrong about me. Actually, he was more honest with me than I've ever been with myself." He lifted a finger to delay her disagreement. "I think if I'm gonna move forward—if I'm ever gonna really live my life and love with all my heart and not just a small part of it… I've gotta face my own demons. And fight them."

James pointed down the tunnel toward the tomb. "That was me, but I'm never going back."

The lantern brightened sharply. The flame within spun wildly. The earth quaked, and the walls cracked. Dust and shards of stone fell onto James and Mary. She held onto him. He crouched over her, holding the lantern toward the broken past. A burst of orange and blue energy flashed from the lantern and down the crooked hall. With a deafening roar, the corridor collapsed behind them, and a tidal wave of earth rushed in their direction. James and Mary screamed in unison as the chaos approached them. The lantern dimmed again, and the last of the stone and earth fell only feet away from their huddled bodies. A burst of musty air rushed past, and dust covered them from head to toe.

They coughed through the filth and clamored away from the debris, brushing themselves off, unwilling to speak through the tainted air. Quickly they found themselves struggling to walk up an incline. The walls drew closer. The ceiling lowered. James pushed Mary ahead of himself, still snorting out dust.

"Look!" Mary wheezed.

James squinted over her head at a dull, gray light not far ahead. As soon as he saw it, the lantern was a map again in his hand. They stooped low to a crawl toward the light, the ceiling slumping and the walls almost touching both of James' shoulders. The growing sense of confinement compelled them on. Though nothing pursued them, their courage threatened to fail. The surging light beyond forced their eyes closed. The tunnel steepened. Mary scrambled on her hands and knees. James sank to his belly. His heart pounded. His breath shallowed.

Mary climbed into the open and bent over to help James up. "Come on!"

"It's tight." James' head spun as he extended his arms up and into the cool air. He set his feet and relaxed his shoulders to squeeze through the small window and strain upward. His eyes adjusted while he pushed down on the ground and dragged his hips through the tunnel's open mouth.

James rolled onto his back and gasped for the clean air. Mary sat beside him and brushed pebbles from her clothes. James coughed forcefully to remove the dust; he shook his head to remove the stress.

"Can we stay above ground now?" No humor graced Mary's voice.

"I really hope so." James wheezed before gulping more air. He lay flat against hard soil. The back of his head protested. "Boy, my head is taking a beating today."

A white haze above masked a sky that could deliver no blue through the crowded atmosphere. He waited for a moment for luminescent particles to float across his vision, but the air had only room for a fog that barely moved.

James stretched to sit up straight and looked at Mary. She glanced about like unwelcome company wasn't far away. James turned his head slowly and found no kind direction. Only barren ground rested under the haze. The source-less light struggled from all directions to fall onto this desolate place and had little success.

"Any idea where we are?" Mary's body language betrayed her discomfort with their surroundings. She was too busy watching for threats to make eye contact.

"No idea at all." He admired her amber eyes, the only natural splash of color in sight, her purple shorts obscured by layers of dust.

"Can the next place we find be a nice house with a warm bed and maybe a hot meal?" Her trademark banter did nothing to settle her countenance.

"Mary..." James waited for her gaze. He leaned close to her and gathered her hand. "It's okay."

She shed a tear. "I know. Of course, I know that. I'm fine." Her lips drew back, and her voice shook. "I'm okay. Everything is fine." More tears flowed. A sob followed.

James slid close and held her in his arms. "You've been so brave. You've stuck by me through so much. My issues, my mistakes, my battles… You've been a faithful friend." He leaned back to look into her eyes. "I don't think I could've made it this far without you."

She forced a weak smile.

"My chances were forty percent at best, right?"

Mary laughed through her tears. "Yeah, you were somewhere between a lost cause and a long shot."

"Hey, you said it. Our success is guaranteed now. Thank you, Mary."

She wriggled out of his embrace and stood up quickly. "Okay, okay. Let's go get that success then. We've got someone to find."

James threw his feet under himself and extended his knees and back with a grimace. Into his peripheral vision a floating trail of orange and blue pointed through the fog. He slipped the map into his pocket and watched the smoke and flame hurry up and forward.

He grinned and cut his eyes at Mary, who was watching the silent guiding light. "On we go."

As they strolled in the map's decided direction, the fog made way before them, just enough to see a few steps ahead. The air stood still, but the muted sound of wind moaned around them. Mary walked close enough to brush against James' arm every few steps.

"What are you gonna say to her when you find her?"

James stared ahead with his brows low. "I don't have a speech planned. I don't think it was ever about having the right words. I think it was about showing up. That's my plan… to show up."

He coughed out what he hoped was the last of the dust in his lungs. Then he realized that the person beside him was the person he should ask. "What would *you* say to her?"

"I don't know…" She took his hand. "But if I were *her*… Yeah, I'd want to hear a lot of groveling. Pitiful, embarrassing, uncomfortable begging." She gave his arm a tug. "Just *don't* make excuses."

James beamed. "I'm fresh out of those."

A burst of air descended upon them from overhead and sent a shiver over James' skin. Like a ripple in a pond the air rushed outward over the dry ground and chased away the fog in every direction. The dull cloud cover remained to keep the light at bay.

They stopped. James locked his gaze in the direction of the map's will, waiting to see what was next. Mary clung to his side and scanned the horizon. The haze rolled farther from their sight and revealed nothing but miles on end of sterile wasteland—except at the center of James' focus.

Miles away, a single mountain stood, a speck of hope in the distance.

"Mary, do you see it?"

She followed his line of sight and strained her eyes. "I see… something. Is that a mountain?"

"I think so," he said, his voice even and calm. "That's where she is."

"Are you sure?"

"I'm sure. This is it."

The earth vibrated under their feet. They stood still and waited until the tremor died after a few seconds.

"Nope, not a fan of that," Mary muttered.

"It's okay." James strode on.

Another vibration grew to a rumble and then a great quake. James fell forward onto his stomach. Mary tumbled backward. The quake grew more violent still.

"Mary!" James crept toward her, his knees jarring against the unforgiving ground.

"I can't!" The earth tossed her up and down in place.

An ear-splitting crack. A great roar. The ground split between them, and the earth rushed apart, beating their bodies as a chasm formed in the desolation.

The rumbling waned and ceased. James jerked his head right and left. The earth was divided as far as he could see. The massive fissure separated them so far from each other that he had to raise his voice to reach her.

"Mar—!" His voice caught. "Mary, are you all right?" A lump rose in his throat.

She groaned and lifted herself onto her elbow. Her eyes gaped when she saw the distance between them. "No!" She bolted up and raced toward the edge.

"No, Mary!" he screamed. "No... It's too far." He lowered his head to the ground. "God, please..."

"What are we gonna do? I don't want to be alone again!" Fresh tears streaked her face.

"It's okay. I'm not gonna let that happen! We'll walk together in one direction until we find a way across. It's gonna be fine." He buried his head in his hands and dug his fingernails into his scalp. "It's gonna be okay, Mary!"

When James looked up again, Mary was flexing her fingers in front of her face.

"Something's wrong... Something's wrong!" She sobbed.

"It's okay, Mary! I'm right here!"

James stared at her in disbelief as he watched pale, gray light pass through her hands, the outlines of her fingertips barely visible.

"What's happening to me?" she pled as the prevailing light traced up her arms and moved from her feet to her knees. "I'm disappearing!"

The whole of her body illuminated from behind, like a cloud trying to cover the sun, only her amber eyes unfazed.

Oh, God.

"It's okay, Mary! It's gonna be okay." He choked on his breath. "Mary, I love you!"

Sadness filled her eyes, but love filled her voice. "Daddy?"

He strained to keep his tear-filled eyes open. "Yeah, baby, it's me."

A radiant twinkle swept through her being, and she was gone.

"No... No, You can't take her..."

A moan of grief emerged from James' soul and crumpled him onto the ground. His body heaved. His hands drew to his aching gut. He lay trembling, broken. But his shattered heart told him to reach into his chest pocket. James forced his will into his body. He reached with a quivering hand, unfastened the button, and pulled out a photograph. Using his palm to push himself onto his knees, he sat up and unfolded the picture.

There beside Gloria and Mary stood James.

SIXTEEN

How long James had stared at the photo, he couldn't tell. Its surface was streaked by tears, and the edges had begun to wrinkle. The man he used to be stared back at him with his arm around his little girl. But something was different. Though he couldn't find a visible distinction, he knew in his soul that he would be able to recognize this photo if side by side with the copy in Gloria's album at home. There was an invisible joy present on his face. His relationship with the girl in this photo was real—it was alive. And now she was gone.

He had spent days developing a closeness with his daughter that he'd never earned before. He had opened his heart and exposed the ugly truth inside, only to lose the one who had stood by him while he faced it all.

He allowed his surroundings to enter his consciousness again. The light of the wasteland hadn't changed. No passage of time was evident. Before him lay a jagged chasm, behind him a mountain he didn't want to face alone. Stuck between the failure of the past and an uncertain future, James wondered if his guaranteed success had vanished with little Mary.

A steady orange blaze streamed out of his pocket and flowed around his body, pointing, he knew, to a place that would require more strength than he had. James mentally tracked his nervous system up and down his arms and legs and then up his back. His muscle and bone told him that he was old; his mind told him that he was weak.

He sent the signal to his body to stand but received no response. He gazed up at the spot where little Mary had begged not to be alone. Her tears filled his vision; her sobs filled his ears.

He offered a quiet thought to the cold atmosphere. "I just lost my best friend."

A sudden gust of wind tore past him and ripped the photo from his fingers. It sailed under his arm and pulled his body around to see where it had gone. The photo skipped on the ground and settled as the gust expired, a fleck of color under the distant mountain.

He coached himself to his feet and grunted to his full height. His body pled with him to rest, but his heart dragged him toward the photo. He trudged forward with no regard for the mountain, his focus on the only piece of little Mary that remained. His posture weary, his body aching, he slid his feet over the cold, hard ground until he reached his only valuable possession.

He bent at his back and stretched down to pin the photo to the ground with his fingertips, but before he could reach it, a subtle breeze nudged it forward a few feet. He staggered forward, still bent. When he arrived at the picture, again it caught the breeze and skidded another few yards away. James growled out in frustration as he loped to the photo and pounced onto his knees to grab it. A powerful gale snatched the photo into its strength and whisked it high and far, spinning wildly and gliding ahead swiftly until it vanished from his sight.

James wrapped his arms around the pangs of grief in his stomach. The orange and blue energy swept under his nose and whipped forward with a burst of urgency, calling him back on course. Anger flooded his mind and body, and before he realized what he was doing, he snatched the map from his pocket and hurled it into the air. Another mighty gust lifted the map and unfolded it to its full width and height. Off it flew like an untethered kite. Soaring, tumbling, diving, it hurried away from him toward the mountain.

Oh, no!

James lurched into a lumbering run. The map spiraled and rolled. He bounded faster until fatigue faded from his mind and determination overtook the pain. The map nosedived onto the ground and dragged forward, slithering left and right. James drew close enough to swipe at it, but his hands were too slow for the erratic wind. Up the map rocketed again and hovered onward over his head. James ran under his guide and leaped to grab it time after time.

"I'm sorry!" he called. "I need You!"

The wind died at last and left the map to float gently into his open hands. James fell to one knee and gasped for air. His heart throbbed vigorously to catch up, each beat pumping grief back to the front of his mind. The map begged him toward the mountain. He looked up to find it no larger, no closer. He folded his guide and tucked it away.

James lowered his eyes again, and they stopped on an object resting on the ground a few yards ahead of him. Its color was so close to the gray earth, that he struggled to decipher its shape.

James welcomed the distraction and allowed his curiosity to bring him to his feet and over to this interruption in the vast, flat waste. He shuffled on until the object was under his nose, but its identity remained a mystery.

He squatted and traced the rounded surface with his eyes. The object protruded from the ground like an archway with no opening, bending over and cupping inward like a bowl. He brushed it with his fingers and then flinched backward when he realized what he touched.

A pelvis?

He stood and swept the landscape before him with his curiosity. About fifty paces ahead another object lay on the dense, thirsty soil. He approached it and discerned from a distance that a femur had caught his eye. Again, he scanned and found another bone, a shoulder blade. He walked on, swaying side to side. A ribcage, a foot, a skull—more and more skeletal remains dotted the area. Some sat above ground; some peeked from underneath. A fresh look across the horizon revealed a sea of death, the earth telling a story he didn't want to know.

James' stomach ached with uncertainty. The farther he walked, the more he had to adjust his gait to find spaces to set his feet. His hair raised with the loudening whisper of a wind he couldn't feel. Was it wind or breath? The bones of a hand crunched under his step. As he looked down, its dusty remnants scattered into the air. The map called him still to the mountain.

James' heart threatened to break in his chest. Little Mary's disappearance replayed in his mind. His daughter waited for him beyond a wasteland so vast he couldn't imagine the distance or time it would take to traverse. Then a mountain would dare him to climb. Even at his destination, face to face with his only child, he had no words that would open a door of favor back into Mary's heart.

Little Mary's words haunted him. *What are you gonna say to her?*

"She wants me to leave her alone…" A tear rolled to his quivering lip. "And I won't even do that."

James looked down to choose his footing carefully and high-stepped over an almost fully intact skeleton, only its jaw obviously absent.

"She hates me with all her heart…" He crushed a collarbone. "And I can't just let her live her life."

He grimaced and stomped a spine, demolishing several vertebrae. "Am I even doing this for her… or am I just trying to relieve my own guilt?"

He lowered his shoulders and dragged his feet through the massive, pale graveyard. Each step was more unstable. The ground became indistinguishable from the bones. No sense of urgency stirred within him. His steps began to slide. Then they began to sink. The bones crumbled and shifted. His feet fell below ground level. He choked on his tears and leaned forward to move himself along with the help of his hands. The more he moved, the more the bones gave way. All solid ground was a memory. His traction failed. His progress faded. James lay onto his stomach and sobbed into his folded arms.

He thought back to his own words and actions that the woods had recalled for him. He had been the father that ignored his child and pushed her away over and over again, always too busy, always too tired.

Always too selfish.

He had looked into his own eyes as he berated his daughter

and made her feel small. His father's insecurity and bitterness were in that cold stare.

She hates me like I hated him.

Again, he imagined Gloria suffering through the pain and weakness of her cancer, and he was too busy hiding from his own pain to be present through hers.

I hate myself… I don't deserve to finish this, and the one who needs me hates me anyway.

James let his tears fall over the bones beneath him and allowed his own joints to become rigid. He lowered his eyelids and breathed deeply, relaxing his muscles into total surrender.

"So…" A gruff voice pierced through his indifference.

James sleepily pulled up his head and neck with great effort. A weathered man with thick brows and silver hair sat on a familiar ornate stone bench a few yards in front of him.

"It looks like you could use a friend."

James offered him no welcome and made no attempt to disguise his despair. "I'm done." He lowered his head into his folded arms again.

"Hmm, I don't think you're done. You haven't found her yet… and you haven't ended up like these people." The strange warrior seemed unfazed by James' posture and tone of defeat. "You still have work to do."

"I'm done," James repeated with a muffled whisper.

"A lot of people stop here… when they're so close."

This brought James' eyes up again with a frown, his chin and neck coated with gray dust. "Close? Does this look close to you?"

The man chuckled. "Very close." His smile showed no regard for James' furrowed brows. "There's nothing keeping you from her." He nodded over his shoulder. "Nothing that isn't in your mind."

James' annoyance sent his voice on a rollercoaster. "Nothing keeping me, huh? Not a gigantic desert that might just be an endless ocean of death. Not a mountain that's miles away. Not the fact that every time I move I sink deeper into this hell. Nothing at all. It's all in my head."

The man cut his eyes left and right over the massive grave. "People have a lot of reasons to quit where you are... to stop short of becoming the person they were made to be. I'd say by your current posture that you've found yours."

James sighed and stared at the space between the bones and the bench's hovering legs. "I'm tired of trying to be someone I'm not. I don't deserve to be the man that she needs."

"Ah, so you know."

He looked at the man. "Know what?"

He smiled again. "The reason you stopped moving forward is because you're not willing to forgive yourself."

"Forgive myself... Why would I do a thing like that?"

"Because *she* needs to forgive you. And you'll never reach her until you forgive yourself."

James surveyed the death around him and beneath him and shook his head. "I turned my back on the people who needed me the most. My place is here." He whimpered. "I'm so tired."

"It would be a shame if you didn't finish the journey that Gloria started."

Offense curled James' lip. Anger stirred within him. "What did you say?"

The man's tone hardened. "What, do you think that Gloria wasn't chasing Mary? Do you think she didn't struggle after what mattered most? Do you think that she's never been *here* before, fighting for her life, for her faith, so that she could fight for *Mary*... so that she could fight for *you?*"

James lay stunned as new tears welled over his vision.

The man stood, somehow on top of the bones, and stared down at James. Smoke and fire swirled in his eyes. "Are you going to let her dreams die in this grave, James?"

James clenched his teeth and pushed up onto his elbows, staring back at the man.

"Well?" the man bellowed. He swung his leg low and fast through the sea of bones, sending smaller bones flying through the air. He crouched and leaned toward James with his fists balled. "You're not the man you were before you jumped into that river. Now *get up!*"

James lowered himself to gather his strength and drew his legs close to his chest. With a low yell he surged up, leaping out of the mire with tremendous force. To his surprise, he landed on his feet, on the cold, gray earth. The man was gone. The bench was gone. He spun around and found not a single bone in sight.

He caught his breath and fixed his eyes on the mountain ahead.

"I'm sorry, God." The map's river of orange and blue flew forward. James closed his eyes. "I'm sorry, Gloria."

He bolted into a sprint.

SEVENTEEN

James gained speed quickly. He squinted as the air whipped by him and chilled his ears. The dry ground rushed under and behind him. Only the mountain interrupted the horizon. And it was coming closer.

He slowly released his scowl of determination and allowed a wide smile to fill his face. "Woohoo!" His victorious cry soared on the air, and the blue and orange fiery smoke twisted, rolled, and dove all around James and raced out in front of his thundering steps. His pace was swift, but his breathing was deep and slow.

I'm not even tired!

He laughed and held out his hands to allow the cool air to refresh his skin. He looked down his arms and found the luminescent particles that were previously absent from this atmosphere swirling over his body, spiraling over his hands, and ducking in and out of his fingers. His heart raced with excitement, void of fear. The discouragement that strangled his faith moments before had evaporated. Joy filled his heart. Hope drove him closer. The mountain grew rapidly before him and rose overhead. In what seemed like moments, the expanse of emptiness lay almost entirely in his wake.

The cloud cover darkened as James reached the start of the incline that would lead him to his goal. The dull light that covered the wasteland weakened as he slowed his pace, the mountain's face taking shape and revealing a winding path through rough, jutting cliffs. Though his steps led upward, no hesitation tempted his mind. The farther he jogged, the more jagged edges and towers filled the landscape that seemed to oppose him. The path banked sharply right and then left, weaving up the side like a snake stalking a would-be victim at the summit. With every step, the steep grade proved more challenging and finally slowed James to a steady march. No signs of life were evident on the mountainside, but massive dead thorn bushes began to encroach on the path along with occasional ashen trees spreading their branches overhead with ill will. The path's steep angle challenged his progress while the gnarled, lifeless trees cast shadows that chased him on.

The clouds swirled dark and anxious. A wind with a low voice called from the peak. A faint scent of sulfur caught James' attention. A strange evil lay ahead, but nothing would keep him from Mary.

The mountain's sharp features smoothed. The path blended into the steepening slope, and soon the only way forward was up. The map confirmed this with rolling blue vapors. Up James trudged without fatigue, just sure steps of power and purpose.

A broad plateau revealed its shape at the top of this world. The bank steepened further, and he had to climb with strong lunges and the support of his hands. In a moment, James would reach the top.

Courage coursed through his body. His energy still glided high. His faith soared far above his diminishing doubt.

No matter what waits at the top of this mountain, I'm going to show up. I'm here to stay.

He dragged himself to the end of what he could see and paused before peering over the edge. Fear was absent from his heart, but having no idea what he would find above, James wished there was a way to prepare himself. Then he remembered that there was a way. He pressed his palms against the last few inches of familiar terrain.

"God…"

No other word entered his mind. A jarring sense of unworthiness flooded James' being. In the grave that almost devoured him, he had been sure that he didn't deserve to help Mary. *And I wasn't wrong about that.* But a realization now stood facing that thought, a truth that kept him from buckling in defeat. Grace. There was grace from God that overcame his weakness, his failure.

"I know I don't deserve another chance. I have done nothing to earn my way here, and I'll do nothing to earn my way back into Mary's heart. I want to help her, but if I've learned anything in this place, I've learned that I can't do anything without You." He gazed through the foreboding clouds to the best heaven he could form in his mind's eye. "She doesn't need me as much as she needs You. But You've brought me here. I've come to this moment for a reason. So, I'm going to do my best, God. I don't know what's next… but I really believe that Your grace is enough."

He closed his eyes until a wave of pure peace passed through the whole of his body and settled in his chest. "Any advice?"

Warmth radiated from his pocket and pulled his hand to the map. He produced it slowly, noticing that the smoke and fire had withdrawn. The heat forced him to switch the map from hand to hand as he unfolded it. Then shock glued his hands to the edges of the parchment.

Blank.

"Uh… Am I miss—?"

A flash of brilliant orange and a rolling black line. A tiny flame traced the paper surface and left smoking ink in its path. James felt pressure wander across the page, tugging at his grip. An unseen hand wrote a message before his eyes in beautiful, fiery calligraphy. One word skillfully crafted appeared across the otherwise empty space, and once finished, the flame retraced the ink and left a pulsing glow.

"Stand," James read. He nodded and basked in the peace that still lingered within him. "I think I can do that." He whispered his gratitude and returned the cooling parchment to his pocket.

James blew out a quick breath and peeked over the edge. His eyes found a wide meadow under the low, dull light. Lush, green grass covered the level ground, except the sprawling patches of wildflowers of various colors and the proud, leafy hardwoods scattered over the scene. The summit boasted life to the edge of the mountaintop and stopped there, not a runner of grass daring to venture over the side. The map released a rolling flame that summoned him up and over.

James climbed with a groan onto the surface and crouched over the grass. The area before him was small and round, perhaps a five-minute walk from edge to edge. Mary was not in sight, so he stilled his breath and tuned his ear beyond the low wind. No other sound presented, but a small grove of hardwoods at the plateau's center requested investigation.

She's gotta be in there.

James rose and strolled warily toward the grove. The smell of flowers mingled with sulfur to make an unpleasant combination. A small, placid pond on one side of the plateau completed the strangely beautiful parcel. He darted his eyes back and forth. Though courage kept his spirit strong, his experience in this world had taught him to expect the unexpected. The moaning wind brushed through the grass and wildflowers and nudged the hardwood branches as he approached the grove which was too dense to see through.

James looked down and found no heading from the map. His heart kept his feet in motion as he entered the edge of the small forest. He zigzagged through the outermost trees and sidestepped, until he spotted Mary hovering ahead. James hurried toward her with a swell of concern. He reached a tree line and found her at the center of a sizeable clearing. The twisted vines of thorns held her up and wove around her frame, writhing restlessly.

A few steps into the clearing, a thorny vine lashed at him from Mary's side, scraping his arm. Another vine struck from her other side, forcing James to backpedal and duck behind a tree. The vines guarded the wide berth of the clearing with brutal vigilance and some keen sense.

He glued himself to the back of the hardwood and called out. "Mary! It's me!" He lightly touched the bleeding scrape across his arm.

James waited for a response but received none. He leaned right to peek around the trunk but was met with a violent whip that rattled the branch closest to him and sent a flurry of leaves fluttering to the ground.

"Mary! Hang on, Mary. I'm coming in!"

James faked left, inducing another vine thrash and then darted from the other side of the tree, bolting toward Mary. The vines above and below her jerked to life and took turns lashing out at him. He ducked under one, leaped over another, and rolled onto the grass before launching himself forward again. He raced with all his might while the vines seemed to regroup.

"Mary!"

The closer he drew, the more confused he became. She hovered with her eyes closed, crying softly, her face turned away from him. He slowed when he realized that she was not commanding the thorns to assail him.

"Mary…"

Sadness washed over him, and the attack faded from his attention. A vine whip smacked his face and spun his head. He staggered backward. Another swept his feet from beneath him, and he lost his breath with a thud on the ground. A vine towered over him like a viper positioning to strike and fell swiftly to crush him, but he rolled out of the way and sprinted for the edge of the clearing. Before he could use a tree for cover, a thick vine coiled around his torso and reeled him back, whipping his head forward. It spun him closer and squeezed him tightly. James yelled as thorns pierced his flesh. He gasped for air under the powerful pressure. The vine lifted him and held him in front of Mary, only a few feet away.

James groaned as the thorns dug deeper. "Mary, I'm sorry," he wheezed. He grabbed the vine and tried to free himself. "I'm gonna help you!"

Mary's eyes remained closed. Tears flooded her cheeks.

"Mary, please lis—"

In a flash the vine ripped itself from around James' body, dragging the thorns across his chest and back and spinning him like a top. He flew like a ragdoll, his shirt shredded open, and crashed in a heap on the ground. Blood trickled from his wounds as he lay disoriented, his face contorted.

"Rough day?" said a cold, calm voice.

James twisted his head in the direction of the words. Green eyes shone through the harrowing dusk.

"If I didn't know better, I'd say you weren't ready for this, friend."

Zell sauntered from the other side of the clearing and walked by Mary without a glance. The vicious vines paid him no interest. He stepped close, nudged James with his toes, and squatted over him. "I can't say I hate to see you like this."

James stared a hole through him.

Zell's face was set like stone. "So, is there a limit to how many times you can let her down?"

James scrambled to his hands and knees and lunged at Zell who kicked the side of his head and sent him back to the grass on his stomach.

He tried to lift his head but laid it back down in throbbing pain, unable to focus his eyes.

"Wow, that felt good!" Laughter permeated Zell's admission.

James rolled onto his back to look up at Zell's face. His blurry vision cleared in time to see a hateful grin.

"So, I see you've misplaced someone." Zell's chuckle ducked in and out of his words.

James seethed silently.

"Actually, James… you've surprised me. Imaginary friends

aside, you never should have made it this far without Gloria. Maybe that'll give you some comfort as you watch your *real* little girl die."

James bolted upright, but Zell swung low with a right hook and laid him down again. His cheek began to swell. Past the lump in his throat, he forced out the question he didn't want to ask. "Who are you, really?" It took all of his breath.

Zell bent low again with a harsh whisper. "*Great* question."

James' eyebrows twisted in anguish. A chill traveled his spine.

"I have many names. And I bet you don't have the courage to utter *any* of them."

Through trembling lips, James blurted, "Let her go!"

"What... this?" He gestured flippantly to the thorns twisting around Mary. "These vines? These nasty little thorns? Oh, that's not me." He laughed loudly. "I'd like to take credit, but *this*... this is *all* Mary." He turned his gaze to her defenses. "You know, it's amazing what a broken heart and a twisted mind can do." He kicked James' side, initiating a coughing fit. "*Really* though... *You* deserve some credit, too. Aren't you the reason she's so withdrawn... so guarded..." He suppressed a deep, dark chuckle. "...so angry?"

Zell stomped James' midsection and laughed. "You know what it's like to be just like daddy, James." He howled his delight.

James curled into a ball and wheezed. He stretched his neck to look at Mary, suspended by the power of those wretched vines, unable to respond to the scene that unfolded before her.

James regulated his breathing while Zell's laugh settled into a sigh. "I'm not that man anymore."

Zell bent over, grabbed James' biceps, and lifted him up with extended arms. James' feet dangled just above the grass. Zell was suddenly taller and stronger.

"Enough fun." Zell's voice was deeper and distorted. "You think you can take a swim in that river and just undo it all? You think you can face me and live?"

Before James' eyes, Zell's face blistered and waved. Patches of his copper skin receded like burning paper, revealing a black, scaly hide. James winced and curled his nose. The smell of sulfur turned his stomach.

Zell tossed James behind himself effortlessly. He tumbled violently and rolled to a stop just short of the edge of the clearing. He lay on his side, his limbs tangled, his back facing Zell.

James fought for consciousness. He rolled his eyes around, looking for his equilibrium. His bones ached. His skin stung. His body cried for relief, for rest, but the single word written in flame on the parchment in his pocket stood branded in his mind.

Stand, James.

He willed himself to sit up and then to stand, stretching through the pain. He reached his full height with his back still turned on his nemesis.

Zell grunted, and a thud rattled the ground. "You know... I was going to make you watch, but I've lost my patience."

James could hear Zell step closer to him—and the sound of something heavy dragging on the ground.

God, strengthen me.

James turned and bristled. Zell's skin and hair were gone. A glistening armor of scales covered his muscular form, and a long heavy tail like a crocodile's rested behind him. Only piercing green eyes were left of the Zell he had known.

The monster held out his hands like he was gripping an invisible orb in front of his chest, and a dark red flame materialized in the space surrounded by his fingers.

"Goodbye, James." Zell whirled around and hurled the flame at James with fierce effort and a thunderous roar.

EIGHTEEN

James watched the approaching attack without a hint of alarm. Like a javelin it whistled through the air toward a fearless man. Just before the fiery projectile arrived, he threw up his forearm in front of his chest. *Thump, thump, thump,* three objects stopped in midair with the sound of dense wood, an inch from James' arm. Three large, black darts, smoldering with a red glow, hovered over his skin, while a black venom spread outward over thin air. An invisible barrier held the threat away from James. He closed his fist and flexed his forearm to find himself attached to a shield.

He held the shield high and then snatched it downward. The darts flew to the ground, and James watched them dissolve into ash before looking up to meet Zell's eyes.

Zell smiled even more broadly than before and reached deep for a low, gravelly voice that slithered through his long, razor-sharp teeth. "You're a fool… a fool out of his depth." He sunk his scaly brows. "You have no idea how strong I am."

James looked past him at Mary who still hovered motionless. A graceful stream of smoke and flame rose from his pocket and swirled into his attention. He took a deep breath and looked again into the eyes of hell.

James' tone was calm and sure. "I went to church for twenty years. I heard my wife pray every day. I even read your favorite book."

Zell bared his teeth. His eyes glinted.

James smirked and raised his voice. "I may not know your strength, but I know your place."

With his left hand, James reached into his pocket for the map. Instead, his fingers slid past a metal pommel and fell on a leather grip. He latched on and pulled with all his might. With a growl, he thrust a long sword over his head. He gazed up at a double-edged weapon sewn together with pure light. He twisted the hilt. Words of living fire were etched over the blade's entire surface, and the point gleamed against the brooding clouds above. Orange flames raced up and down the glowing, blue edge.

James looked back at Zell, whose countenance and demeanor had changed.

He's afraid.

James lowered the sword in front of himself and held the invisible shield to his side, his jaw set and his eyes daggers.

Zell lowered his body to the ground like a hungry lion. He darted his eyes around the clearing. The leaves of the trees turned to ash in a wave of instant drought. Every trunk and branch shriveled and shed its color. Knots and bark cracked. Joints popped. The grass beneath them vanished, leaving the ground hard and barren.

James widened his stance and pushed off his heel. He bounded toward Zell. The dark creature bolted away from him on all fours, past Mary and out of the clearing. James slowed and stopped near Mary.

What are you doing?

The trees around them shifted and creaked. The ground rumbled softly. Branches stretched toward James. He adjusted his grip on his weapon and widened his stance, ready for battle, but the trees halted their progress long before reaching him. He waited, listening to his own breath.

The thorny vines around Mary drew his gaze. They slowly retracted and unwound from her body. Countless faint scar lines etched her skin. The vines under her kept her in suspension while the rest assumed a new purpose. They chased each other through the air in wide circles. Over, under, and around they hurried and thickened to form a spherical cage. In a moment, every exposed space around her was filled, and James could see Mary no more.

He drew in his lips and drew back the sword to free her, but the ashen trees began twitching and jolted into violent motion. Branches soared over his head, and the ground shook again. James spun around to see which branch would strike first.

The roots beneath him made the first move, bursting through the cracked earth. One slammed into his side and sent him stumbling. Another darted in front of his knees before he could steady himself. He toppled into a somersault and rolled back onto his feet in time to slice the sword of light through a swooping branch. He whirled and severed an advancing root. More branches soared downward and met a similar fate. He swiped and stabbed at another root when from the corner of his eye he saw Zell descending from above. The monster twisted as he fell toward James and whipped his massive tail around, aimed at James' head.

James let out a low yell as he lunged at Zell with the sword overhead. Terror filled Zell's eyes. James had outmaneuvered him. His powerful stroke separated Zell's tail from his body in one motion. Zell crashed onto the ground, shaking the earth, and his tail flopped and wriggled beside him.

Zell looked up and roared toward the sullen clouds. The trees, branch and root, flew at James from every direction, all at once. James held the sword outward and howled as he swung it all around his body. A blast of fiery energy shot from the point and sent a devastating wave of power around the perimeter of the clearing. James stumbled to his knees and watched as every attacker fell lifeless. A bright orange cutting line glowed through the clearing, lighting up the dusk. The top half of every trunk of the forest's trees toppled.

Every piece of wood from branch to root crumbled into white ash. A cloud of dust billowed over the clearing, running across the ground and soaring into the air. James kneeled with his eyes closed, his breath suspended, and his heart pounding. He listened closely for Zell's next move with the shield over his head and the sword pulled behind his back. Ash gathered on his skin. Tension gathered in every muscle.

A light breeze cascaded through the now open landscape, and James cracked his eyes and watched the air clear with his gaze fixed in the direction he'd last seen Zell. The spaces where his body and tail had been were barely invaded by the remnants of the disintegrated forest. The ash settled slowly. He searched all around himself. No footprints. Only the cage of thorns was close.

He eased himself upright and scanned his surroundings again. The shell that encased Mary was the only cover that Zell could use. James snorted ash from his nostrils and sprinted around the vines to confront him. He arrived again where he started without incident. His enemy had flown.

The cage before him remained still, serving its purpose of protection. Beyond his breathing, James could hear faint whimpering from within the vines. He braced himself in front of the prison and raised the sword, but the vines were moving before he could swing. In circular motion they retracted from their places, unraveling the bubble that shielded her from James' conflict with Zell.

James stood on guard, ready to take on her thorns, this time armed and mighty. Mary's face reappeared, tracked with tiny scars and wet with tears. She hovered over the mountain with her eyes still closed. The vines that had surrounded her twisted around her arms and torso as they were before, making no threat to harm James.

A violent, icy wind swirled around them and stirred up dust and ash into a haunting haze. Then a sound that James knew well crept into the clearing, the sound of labored breathing. A distant muttering of lies and hate grew louder. A fine dust of orange and blue exploded from the sword and permeated the atmosphere around them.

Surrounded again. Voices beyond numbering lumbered toward them from every direction, their gaping mouths moaning, their heads swaying at the end of their feeble, elongated necks. Though James felt a chill travel his spine, no fear seized his heart. He turned his attention to Mary.

The vines lowered her feet to the ground but held her upright. He warily stepped forward, ready for the vines to turn on him. He was allowed to approach without resistance, and he tiptoed in front of her.

"Mary." Tears filled his eyes, and sorrow filled his voice.

James saw no indication that he was heard. He shook off his invisible shield, and it thumped and wobbled on the hard ground. He stretched out his sword and turned its point to his pocket. As he pressed it down into its place, the blade of light gave way, and the hilt slid easily inside and out of sight.

James shuffled even closer and reached toward her hand. The vines twitched and drew back from her arm, poising warily against his approach. He took her hand anyway, and Mary opened her eyes, looking off into another world.

"Hey, baby girl." He mustered all the joy he could find into a weak smile.

Mary produced more tears without a sound. He squeezed her hand, and she blinked.

"Mary, I've been on a long journey lately, and that journey has made me realize that I have failed you. I've spent your whole life hiding from who I had become."

He glanced at the voices marching toward them, still some distance away. The ash continued to stir in the swirling wind.

"I was afraid… I was angry… I was selfish." He blinked away a tear. "I was blind. And I pushed away the two people I loved the most."

The vines around her arm crept toward him. He watched as they passed over her hand and began to crawl up his. He winced through stinging pain as the thorns grazed his skin.

"I was a broken man. In my insecurities and bitterness, I hurt my family. I was a poor husband. And I was not a father to you."

The vines twisted around his arm, crawled over his elbow, and reached toward his shoulder. He looked up and found Mary's amber eyes staring back into his. They were filled with longing, not the coldness he'd come to expect. The vines tightened, and the thorns dug deeper. Blood trickled toward their hands.

James grimaced. "Mary, it won't change what I've done. It won't restore lost time. And it won't give back what I took from you... but I'm so sorry."

She squeezed his hand and wept aloud.

"I'm so sorry, baby."

James wrapped his free arm around her and pulled her close. He wept with her as the vines wrapped around both of their bodies and bound them together.

I can feel her pain. Let her feel my love.

"Mary, the most important thing that I discovered... is that your mom was right... about everything."

The voices murmured only a few yards away.

"You don't need these thorns... You don't have to listen to these voices... You can be free."

She turned her head to look at her father.

"Mary, all you need is God."

The voices cupped their long fingers around their mouths. The thorns wriggled and twitched. A fire burned in Mary's eyes.

NINETEEN

"Dad."

James heard Mary's voice, but her lips were sealed shut. "Mary..."

"Dad," her voice called again, from where James couldn't tell.

"Mary, we need to go. We can't stay here."

"Dad."

"Baby, let's get you somewhere sa—"

"Dad."

The voices were upon them.

"Mary!"

"Dad."

"Mary!"

James sat up and furiously groped for Mary, his heart racing. A blinding light forced him to squint. He struggled to free himself from the vine twisted around his arm, feeling weak, confined to slow motion.

"Mary!" he cried.

Footsteps raced toward him. Garbled voices filled his mind.

A loud beeping sound grabbed his attention.

"Mary…"

"James, you need to calm down."

"Where's Mary?" he slurred. Pain racked his body. Nausea and dizziness overwhelmed him. He closed his eyes and laid back. A hand guided the back of his head to a pillow.

"Easy, James. Is his IV still in?"

"How did it get wrapped around his arm like this?"

"Wha… What's going…" James murmured.

"James, can you hear me?"

"Who…"

"My name is Devin. I'm your nurse today. You were in an accident. We're here to take care of you."

"I…" James felt consciousness slipping from him.

"Don't worry, sir. We're going to make sure…"

* * *

"His injuries aren't life-threatening, and that's a miracle—and I don't use the word 'miracle' lightly. A crash like that never leaves a person in this kind of shape. He'll have a difficult recovery though. He's the definition of 'banged up.'"

James rolled his eyes around behind his shut lids, unable to move any other part of his body. Dull aches emanated from every bone and ligament. Mary rushed to his mind, and a surge of urgency lit his nervous system.

Is she safe?

He tried to move and received sharp pulses of pain for his

effort. He flexed whatever muscles would respond to him—a toe, a thumb, his nose, all of them twitched in succession.

"His scans are clear of significant internal injury. We'll be able to surgically repair his leg soon, and the rest of the breaks should set as they are. Right now, he needs rest and supervision."

"Will he be awake soon?"

Mary.

"How lucid he'll be over the next few days is up to him. He'll come back around when he's ready. His outburst yesterday made pretty clear that you're on his mind. It might do him some good to hear your voice."

Footsteps trailed out of the room. A door closed. Silence succeeded.

I wrecked the car. I drove drunk.

Grief washed over his soul.

Gloria...

He felt tears form and then spill over his cheeks.

"Dad?"

Mary's address jolted his heart. He fought a battle in his mind to move, to show her that he could hear her. He failed to muster the strength.

Was it a dream?

"Dad, can you hear me?"

No, it was too real. It was so hard.

"I'm right here," Mary said.

I'm not the same.

Her hand rested on his. He concentrated on his hand and begged it to move.

"You're gonna be okay, Dad. I'm making sure they take care

of you."

His hand ignored his mind, so he turned his focus to his voice.

"Mom's arrangements..." Her tone weakened. "I'm taking care of everything." She withdrew her hand. "It's okay if you need to rest. Aunt Lucy and Uncle Rick are helping me."

He tried to speak but increased the volume of his breath instead.

"I'm sorry." Her voice was broken. "If I hadn't said what I said..." She whined out a breath, holding back a sob. "This shouldn't have happened."

James pushed the speed of his breathing and searched for momentum to spend every ounce of energy in his body.

Mary whispered to herself. "Why couldn't I be more like Mom?" She turned and walked toward the door.

James strained with his mind, and his body followed. He exhaled a rattling breath. Mary paused. He breathed in deeper and forced out a long groan while he turned his head slightly.

"Dad, can you hear me?"

God, please.

He cracked his lips and released another low groan.

She stepped closer. "Are you trying to say something?"

With another deep breath he sent one broken syllable into the cold hospital room.

"No..."

"Dad?"

"No..."

He flexed the corners of his mouth. His eyelids fluttered. He bent his toes. He fought for every move, every opportunity to show her he was present in that bed, present in that moment.

"No... Mary..."

She stood at his side and gathered his hand. She flinched when he gave her fingers a slight squeeze. "Dad… you're awake."

"No…"

"What do you mean?"

He pried open his eyelids and finally moved his lips in slow motion. "It's not your fault… It's my fault…" he whispered.

"Dad, I–"

"I… was wrong…"

She squeezed his hand and placed it back on the bed. "Dad… we can talk, but you need to rest for a little while." She backpedaled. "Let's do this when you're stronger."

"Mary…"

The door closed.

* * *

"How bad is it?" James lay groggy and weak with his hospital bed inclined and his eyes half shut.

His doctor stared down at James' chart while he spoke. "Not bad at all, all things considered. Your leg needs surgery, and your arm and ribs will take some time. You're going to spend a lot of time doing physical therapy."

"Where is my daughter?"

"I haven't spoken with her in a couple of days, but she's up to speed on your condition."

James grimaced as he leaned onto his elbow and adjusted his position, a choice that wasn't worth the pain that followed.

"James… now that you're awake, police will be coming by

to discuss the nature of your accident... and the results of your blood test that night."

James sighed and nodded. "I understand."

A knock on the door drew their attention, and Mary slipped into the room. James and Mary looked into each other's eyes.

"I'll leave you to it." The doctor strode through the open door.

Mary turned and closed it as slowly as possible. Her shoulders rose and fell before she turned to face her father again. The icy glare he'd seen the last time he watched her enter a hospital room was tucked away. Mary's eyes told a story of grief and exhaustion.

The weight of her trauma filled the room, and James felt small.

"You've been through so much, Mary... and I just piled on top of it all."

She held up a hand and shook her head. "I'm okay."

"I know." He coughed weakly. "You're stronger than I've ever been."

"Dad—"

"Mary, there's something I have to say, and I hope you'll hear me."

When he held her gaze, she took a seat beside his bed. "Okay."

He exhaled his nerves and turned his head to face her. "Mary, I'm sorry. And 'sorry' doesn't go back to the accident. It doesn't go back to Mom's diagnosis... Mary, I'm sorry for everything... the way I treated you your whole life." He stifled a sob. "And I think I owe *you* an apology for how I treated your mom."

Mary's eyes flooded, but her expression didn't change.

"I always thought I was a good enough husband and father because I didn't treat my family like *my* dad treated me... but

I settled for that. I settled so far short of what you needed." He blinked hard to release a pool of tears. "And that was miles from what you deserved."

James swallowed the lump in his throat. "I realize now that I wasn't there for you." He paused to steady his voice and failed. "I'm so sorry I wasn't there."

Mary spoke calmly but with a sharp edge. "You *weren't* there." She closed her eyes and lowered her volume. "And I've come to terms with it. But what I'm really struggling with isn't what I deserve… It's what Mom deserved. And she was the most extraordinary person in the world." Her voice climbed again. "She gave everything. You said *you* sacrificed everything, but *she*…" Mary's tears took her words.

James lowered his head. Mary stood swiftly.

"I should be glad that you're doing some soul searching. No… I *am* glad." She sidestepped away from the bed. "I'm just not in a place where I can help you through it." She walked to the door.

"She was right." James' words reached Mary as she grabbed the door handle.

Mary froze.

"She was right about God."

Mary looked over her shoulder at him with wrinkled eyebrows. "You believe?"

James nodded, pleading with his eyes.

"I'm *really* not ready for that conversation."

James raised a tight-lipped smile through the pain that racked his heart. "Okay, Mary. I'll be here."

Mary stared at him for a moment, opened the door, and disappeared.

James inhaled deeply and laid his head on his right cheek to exhale. His eyes fell on a donated Bible that sat on the bedside table.

He watched as a wisp of blue smoke, traced by an orange flame, lilted from its pages and vanished.

A way forward.

ACKNOWLEDGEMENTS

Thank you, God, for enabling me to do anything worth doing.

Thank you, Maria, for supporting every one of my creative efforts and keeping me grounded through the process.

Thank you, Mom, for lending your writing expertise and positivity.

Thank you, Dad, for believing that I'm much more able than I am.

Thank you, kids, for making sure I'm never too focused.

Thank you, friends and family in the faith, for praying, sharing, and buying in on day one.

A NOTE FROM AUSTIN

This book went from a "one day" dream to a heavy burden a few months ago. I knew that I wanted to tell a story about grief and hope, but there was much more to come that I didn't expect.

I'm a pastor and preacher "by day," and I was surprised by how closely writing fiction compared to writing a sermon. Here are a few examples. An idea or divine inspiration may linger in your mind for months before arriving at the pulpit. A sermon's development can engage your emotions over long periods of time and take your heart for a ride that no one else knows about. It's harder than it seems. The end result always surprises you. And my favorite part is that the sermon is always preached to the preacher before it's preached by the preacher.

Writing this book has challenged me, and it's my prayer that it has challenged you. We should all be motivated to show up for the people that God has placed in our lives, and that can be hard, especially when we don't see the tremendous value in ourselves that God sees.

I want you to deeply know that you and your story matter. God has a plan for your life that doesn't only affect you. Your life is an opportunity to impact more people around you than you realize, and that impact is eternal!

Whatever you do, don't settle for a life without forward progress. There is always a way forward, and you can find the most amazing Guide in the Word of God.

If you're moving, keep going! If you're stuck, it's not too late to get up and take a step.

God loves you, and I'm praying for you.

If this book has been a help to you, please share it with someone else who might be encouraged forward.

You can join my newsletter and stay updated at www.austinmoore.net. You can also find my social media links there!

Until the next book, thank you for reading.

May God be with you!

Made in United States
Orlando, FL
29 August 2023